BlaQue

Published by:

G Street Chronicles
P.O. Box 1822
Jonesboro, GA 30237-1822
www.gstreetchronicles.com
fans@gstreetchronicles.com

Cover design:
Hot Book Covers, www.hotbookcovers.com

ISBN 13: 978-1-9405744-8-6
ISBN 10: 194057448X
LCCN: 2015904536

Dirty
DNA
3
THE RENEGADE

Prologue

I don't remember exactly when I started to hear the voices. Or the one voice I should say. I may have been about four or five years old when Takiya first came to visit me. I was living with Uncle Neko at the time; and although my uncle made sure I didn't want for anything, I knew at such a tender age that something wasn't quite right about the voice I would hear from time to time which got more defined and pronounced the older I got.

Other kids had imaginary friends that they blamed for the bad shit that they did. If those same kids got caught doing something they had no business doing, they would blame their imaginary friend to keep their little asses out of hot water. My imaginary friend was real and she was always up to something.

I had an imaginary friend that never went the fuck home and she was always into something that could get me caught up in a major way. Takiya was the one who did the bad shit and she left me to handle the aftermath! I took more beatings than the good Lord should have allowed for shit I couldn't remember doing, but somehow got blamed for. As I got older, I would remember doing the shit and I would even remember trying to stop Takiya from doing it, but she was always faster, smarter and stronger than me. I had no choice but to do things her way or she would make shit harder for me than it already was back then.

Takiya stayed with me through my childhood right into my pre-teens and she is still here causing more problems than ever. I am eighteen now, and she is more out of control than she has ever been before.

Chapter One

Who I Am
YaYa Nicole

My childhood was typical with the exception of some of the childish things Takiya did just to get a rise out of the little make-shift family I had left. I didn't know much about my mother except what Uncle Neko would tell me about her, which wasn't much. I don't even remember her. She died when I was still an infant. My punk ass father didn't want shit to do with me and that shit was fine by me because from what I understand, he was a nut!

My father was supposed to be some big time rapper from D.C. who went crazy after he was shot. From what I know about the story, he was shot for some shit he didn't have anything to do with. He just had bad luck in the female department and it almost got his ass killed.

Uncle Neko never told me anything about my mother or father while I was growing up and that shit left me feeling incomplete. What I was able to find out about them I had to find out on my own and that shit was hard to do being that we were living in the A and my parents were both born and raised in Washington, D.C. I used to ask Uncle Neko why my father didn't want me. He would tell me that there were some things about my parents that I just didn't need to know. He always preached that the less I knew about them the better off I would be. I didn't know how true that really was. It leads me to believe that my parents were involved in some ill shit and Uncle Neko didn't want me to have anything to do with any of it! He always told me I reminded him of the aunt I was named after, YaSheema "YaYa" Clayton. He would speak so highly about my auntie, but he wasn't too fond of my mother ShaniQua "'NiQue' Watkins for some odd reason.

From the pictures I have of my mother and aunt, I resemble my Aunt YaYa more so than my mother. I had inherited our family's alluring grey eyes and cocky, headstrong attitude as well. The only thing I could tell that I had inherited from my mother – when I looked at her in the pictures – was her fair skin tone.

Even though Uncle Neko, and his snotty ass wife Rhina, most likely had my best interest at heart by keeping what really happened to my mom and dad from me, I felt like there was still something missing. I wasn't complete without knowing why I was going through the things I was going through. I needed to know who I was and where I came from. I needed to know why the crazy things going on in my head were happening. I definitely needed some answers as to what was going on with the voice in my head who called herself Takiya. Takiya was who I liked to call my best friend and my worst enemy all rolled into one. She has been around for as long as I can remember. She went from me hearing her when I was all by myself, to her being around all the time. At first, she didn't make herself known while other people were around; but the older I got, the bolder she became. I think she started really showing off for the attention of it all. Takiya wanted people to notice her instead of them just seeing me. I think it was her way of getting the attention she craved. I know she uses me to get that attention, too.

I haven't told Uncle Neko or Aunt Rhina about Takiya because I know he would look at me funny. Uncle Neko caught me talking to Takiya a few times and he gave me a strange look as if he knew I wasn't talking to myself. I think he knows there is something going on inside my head. He might even know that Takiya is the one I have been talking to, but since he hasn't asked me anything about it, I'm not going to tell him anything about her. Besides, Takiya has told me over and over that if anyone found out about her, they would lock me up in some hospital and they would never let me out.

So instead, I've learned how to control that shit. I had to block Takiya out when Uncle Neko Aunt Rhina or anyone else was around. Actually, I've gotten very good at keeping Takiya my little secret.

I haven't been able to figure out why Takiya doesn't like Aunt Rhina very much. Takiya told me that Rhina doesn't like me either. I don't give a fuck if she does or she doesn't. She just needs to leave things alone if they don't pertain to her nosy ass. Aunt Rhina was always minding my business, and being that she has never birthed anything...she needs to fall back.

I am glad I will be moving out of their house and away from their weird looks. I need to be able to find out who I am and where I came from. I already know that Uncle Neko and Aunt Rhina aren't offering any information, so I know whatever it is they are hiding might explain why I hear the voice of someone who isn't there and no one else can see.

I know finding out about my mother's life will shed some light on the wild shit I got going on inside of me. In order to find out who I am, I have to find out where I came from; and the only person who knows that and may be willing to talk is my father, because Uncle Neko and Aunt Rhina refuse to tell me anything valuable. Since they won't tell me, I'm going to find out what I need to know all on my own even if it kills me.

Chapter Two

YaSheema Nicole

"YaSheema, we need to talk," Uncle Neko said.

I knew he was going to start in on me about going to school at Howard University in Washington, D.C. This was a conversation we had several times in the last past year and I didn't feel like having it again. He was blowing me with his speeches about getting an education and doing something with myself...just as long as it wasn't going to happen anywhere near or around Washington, D.C.

"Wassup, Unc?" I asked him, knowing fully well what he wanted to say before he even started in on me.

"I wanted to know what your plans are when you leave for school tomorrow. I just don't see why you can't go to school down here. There are plenty of great schools right here in Atlanta. You don't have to go to school in D.C. to get a good education; you know. Do you even know what you're gonna major in, or is this just another way for you to ease to that city when

I strictly forbid you to?" Uncle Neko asked me in a serious tone.

How many times is he going to ask you the same ole thing? Takiya asked annoyed.

I played it real cool and paid her no mind. It was something I have gotten so used to doing. She had a bad habit of barging in when she wasn't needed. It was almost like ignoring a whining child after you told them no about something. You just drown them out until they eventually stop. The only problem was Takiya never seemed to just stop. She may quiet down in the background, but she was always lurking, listening and waiting on her queue to turn up and turn shit out.

"Unc, I told you I haven't decided what I want to major in yet. All I know is that I believe my calling is in D.C. Maybe I will try to find my father," I said, waiting for his reaction to my plans. I knew it wasn't going to be good.

Just as I suspected, he wasn't thrilled with my decision to go anywhere near Washington, D.C. The wrinkle lines formed on his forehead and I could bet that the graying hair on his head and face were all because of whatever had happened to our family in D.C. I could read it all over his face. His aging grey eyes fixed themselves on me and he made me uncomfortable with the way he was looking at me.

"I don't think that is a good idea, YaSheema. There is a lot of stuff you don't know about what happened up there and you ain't ready for it yet. I don't see why you can't just go to school down here so you can be with your friends," he said again.

"When would be a good time? You and Aunt Rhina never want to tell me shit about my mother and father! You don't want me to ask you anything about them, and there is no way in hell I should have to walk around through life not knowing who I am or where I come from. You knew your parents. Why can't I know mine?" I whined.

"I think you should watch your mouth and calm your little ass down! Has it ever crossed your mind that we are trying to protect you from all the shit that went on up there? If your father wanted you to know anything about him, you would be with him and not us. There are some things that are better left alone and finding your father is definitely one of them," Uncle Neko said sternly.

I sucked my teeth and rolled my eyes in defiance. He could say whatever he wanted, but I was going to D.C.; with his blessings or without them. It didn't matter to me. He wasn't the one who lived feeling incomplete, unloved and unwanted. I knew even though he had Aunt Rhina, something was missing from Uncle Neko's life. The problem is he wasn't ready to admit it.

"I am only going to say this one time and one time only...there is nothing in that city for you! You can go anywhere you want, but you need to keep your ass out of the District! If you gotta go then fine...but don't go looking for a nigga that don't wanna be found. Got it?" he said.

I nodded my head as though I were in agreement with him. Uncle Neko left my half-packed room and went on about his business. Uncle Neko could say whatever he wanted, but it sure wasn't going to stop me from my mission. For the last eighteen years I have struggled with who I am. I knew exactly how kids who were adopted felt. They felt like a piece of them was missing and only finding the piece that fit into the puzzle would make them feel whole.

Here I was with the scattered pieces and none of them fit.

"I bet his bitch Rhina got something to do with why he doesn't want you to go to D.C. She probably has convinced him that you would never come back if you were to get from up under their old asses!" Takiya laughed.

I got up off the bed and made my way to where my IPod was sitting on top of some of my boxes that I packed to take along with me. I needed something, anything, to drown out Takiya. Her taunting isn't what I needed right now. I turned the music on as loud as I could and tried to focus on getting dressed for my going away party. It was going to be the last time I saw some of my friends from Georgia until I came back home on break.

"So you're going to ignore me? You know Rhina is a bitch. Admit it!" Takiya said, making herself heard over the music.

"I don't have to admit anything. It might not be her. Did you ever think of that? It could be Uncle Neko. There's something in D.C. that he doesn't want me to know about. I don't think it's Rhina," I said, defending my aunt. She wasn't my favorite person, but I didn't want to accuse her and she wasn't the one responsible for the way Uncle Neko was acting.

Takiya settled down after I put her in her place and I continued to get myself ready for my last night out with my small circle of friends from high school. This new chapter in my life was exciting and I was ready to get the show on the road so I could find out who I really was. I knew the answers to all of my questions lived in the heart of the Nation's Capital and I was determined to find them.

Chapter Three

Ronald "Dread" Evans
Lost

"Man, get up! You've been lying around all day. We need to talk," Crack said, standing over top of me with his wife Queen by his side. They were both looking down at me like concerned parents. The female I talked into leaving the bar with me last night was still passed out on the other side of me. I can't even say I knew her name. It really didn't matter because I didn't have any intentions of seeing her again anyway. She was a lousy lay from what I could remember. Either that or I had gotten so shit faced last night that I didn't even remember if the sex was good or not. It didn't matter because the hoe had to go.

I nudged her to wake her and she moaned and rolled over like she didn't want to be bothered; exposing her partially naked body. Queen sucked her teeth and Crack gave me the *we have to talk* look. I nudged ole' girl and she finally sat up.

"Look ahh... shawty, you have to go. My folks got

something to lecture me about," I said, giving Crack the evil eye. I was glad that he had come so I had an excuse to get rid of what's her name, but I didn't feel like being chastised like I was a child.

I sat up and wiped the sleep that had gathered in the corner of my bloodshot eyes. I knew Crack and Queen weren't there on a social visit. It seemed like they were never here on a social visit anymore. They only came around to badger me about shit I didn't think was any of their business. Just because I stayed secluded in the guest house on their property did not give them the right to intrude on my privacy. I paid my rent from my royalties and that's all that should matter.

I looked from Crack to Queen who were both looking at me with so much pity and disappointment in their eyes. I guess if I managed to give a fuck long enough to look at myself in the mirror, I could see why they looked at me with so much disgust. I had let my life go completely downhill. Day in and day out for the past seventeen years it had been the same thing. I would drink, smoke and stay in seclusion. I was living off of the little royalties from the album I released right after the birth of my daughter.

As the thoughts of my baby girl filled my hazy mind, I felt the need to drink. Drinking and smoking were the only things I could do to drown out the guilt I felt every time I thought about what I had done.

After I found out about NiQue and her mental issues and almost lost my life because of the craziness she and her family had involved me in once again, I got ghost. I didn't want anything to do with anyone associated with the Reynolds-Clayton Family. That included my own daughter, YaSheema Nicole. That family was severely fucked up; from the head of their empire Darnell Clayton down to his murderous children. Well, I guess I should say child, because to my knowledge, they were all dead with the exception of my daughter and her uncle Neko. Either way, I wanted nothing to do with any of them. None of them meant me any good and the further away they were from me, the better off I would be.

With thoughts of my crooked extended family fresh on my mind, I reached over to the nightstand in hopes of finishing the bottle of Ciroc I had from the night before; but before I could wrap my hands around the bottle, Queen popped my hand like a mother does her disobedient child. She nodded her head in the direction of the half-dressed woman who was slowly trying to come out of her drunken stupor.

"You deal with this because I can't," Queen said to her husband and threw up her hands in defeat.

My female companion finally got her shit together and exited the guest house with Queen on her heels. I knew Queen wasn't going to be right until the questionable woman was off of her property.

With Queen and my company gone, I was able to reach for the bottle of Ciroc without being judged. Taking a long swig from the bottle, I sat there waiting for Crack to say whatever Queen had sent him to my house to say. Right on cue, Crack started in on me like I knew he would.

"Dunny, how long are you gonna' do this to yourself? You've been doing the same thing for the past seventeen years and you ain't got shit going for you," Crack scolded.

"You haven't recorded anything. You're not even trying to do anything with yourself. Then what's up with your daughter man? I know we went through some horrible shit a few years ago, but you can't keep walking around through life pretending like it didn't happen. Drinking, smoking and fucking these basic bitches isn't gonna' change any of it," Crack continued.

I just kept on taking long gulps of Ciroc that burned the back of my throat, but I knew that burn would be replaced with the euphoric feeling I got when I was high or drunk. That's all I needed and all I wanted.

"You can't keep slowly killing yourself like this."

I didn't say a word to Crack. Instead, I took another long swig from the bottle I was nursing, hoping it would eventually rock me back to sleep. I didn't want to think. I didn't want to feel. I only wanted to drown my sorrows in the bottom of the bottle I was holding.

"See, that's the shit I'm talking about Dread! You're hold up in my fucking guest house. You're bringing basic bitches to my property. You don't know these hoes. You're bringing them too close to my wife and kids. This isn't what we agreed on. We were always in this for the music and the money. Somewhere along the lines, this shit went to the left because you let your dick get you in a bunch of trouble and now you're running away from your past like a bitch. Don't you know that the shit you went through with NiQue, YaYa and even that crazy bitch Pinky should be your motivation to do something? That shit would have made me grind harder for this music shit. Instead, you are in my guest house fucking hoes, drunk, high and not giving a fuck about the people who invested time and money on you. You got my wife breathing down my back. Dread, you know you're my man fifty grand, but I gotta' put my foot down. You're starting to interfere with me getting pussy from my own wife and that ain't gangsta. Look, I know you went through some rough shit back then, but don't let that defeat you."

Crack is lucky he's one of my oldest friends. I wouldn't take anyone talking to me like that except him. I think it hurt more coming from him because everything he said was the truth. I didn't even have a snappy comeback for him. I just sat there gawking at him while I held the bottle. Crack pulled up a chair and cracked open a blunt. My mouth watered as I watched him empty the guts of the cigar into the overflowing wastebasket and repack it with some Purple Haze.

"Dread, I'm working on some new ventures. I want you to get your shit together so you can be a part of them," Crack said, handing me the freshly-rolled blunt.

I didn't hesitate in taking the lit blunt from his hands. "Crack, you know you my boy and everything, but I ain't interested in getting back in the limelight. I think I have had enough of being on stage. I think that's how I got in this mess anyway," I said, taking a long, deep pull of the potent weed.

"I'm not talking about you performing. I'm talking about you doing some voice over work and maybe ghostwriting some projects from some up and coming acts I managed to pull in. In case you haven't noticed, the rest of the world is still moving forward and it's leaving your black ass behind. Come on and get some of this money. Write a few hooks, sell a few rhymes and make a few dollars. No one will even know it's you. You can stay in the background," Crack said.

I took the last sip from my bottle and tossed it to the side. "I don't think I'm ready for all of that. I'll tell you what...I'll think about it. How's that?" I said greedily taking the blunt from Crack.

"Naw man, there is no time to think on it. It's either you're in or you're out. I hate to say it bro, but if you're out, then you're all the way out. That includes my property. Queen isn't gonna' take too much more of your late nights, girls, drugging and boozing. She gave me an ultimatum: either you get your shit together or we both gotta' go and I ain't got any plans on leaving my wife and family because you can't get pass your past."

Now I was furious. Crack was acting like we didn't build Cap Citi together. He was acting like I was worthless. Hell, I paid my rent to stay in their two-bedroom guest house and my checks always cleared when they went to cash them. All that noise he was making wasn't about anything other than him being afraid his wife was going to hold out on giving him some ass.

When he tried to pass the blunt to me, I shook my head in defiance. "Naw... I'm good. If you and Queen want me out, all you got to do is say the word and I'm out," I said, finally getting out of the bed and stumbling to the bathroom. I didn't bother to close the door behind me. Crack could do us both a favor and just leave.

When I finished my business, I fully expected Crack to be gone; but he wasn't. As a matter of fact, he was still sitting in the same spot rolling up another blunt.

"You're still here?" I stammered. The Ciroc early in the day had my head spinning and all I wanted to do was crawl back in my bed and sleep. It was too early for me to be up and it was damn sure too early for me to be going back and forth with Crack over what his wife had said.

"Yeah, I'm still here! The better question is do you still want to be here?" Crack said, standing up. I let out a sigh of relief because from the looks of it, he was done lecturing me and I was glad. Crack walked to the door and took another look back at me and shook his head, and then he walked out, slamming the door behind him so hard that the windows shook.

I lay back on my bed thinking about all that Crack said to me and as much as I hated to admit that he was right, he was. I absolutely hated who I had become. I had turned into an alcoholic loser, and to top it all off, I was a deadbeat. I sat back up and fished around in my nightstand and pulled out the only thing I had left that should have meant something to me. It was a picture of my daughter the day NiQue and I had brought her home from the hospital after she was born. I had long since cut NiQue out of the picture because I didn't want to be reminded of her. I couldn't even look in her face I was so disgusted with her. It was bad enough my daughter looked just like her mother and aunt. She had the very same grey eyes her Uncle Neko and her Aunt YaYa had once possessed.

The picture brought up so many painful memories and my past indiscretions that I tried to mask with alcohol, drugs and sex with random women.

"I'm gonna' do better, baby. I promise. I'm gonna' get my shit together. When I do... hopefully you can forgive me for leaving you. I had no choice. I was hurt. I know it wasn't your fault, but I didn't want to fuck up your chances of having a normal life. Lord knows I seemed to fuck up every single female's life I entered and I didn't want to do the same to you," I mumbled in a drunken stupor.

I slumped back in the bed and dissected the picture

of my daughter who I knew nothing about. I lay there wondering who YaSheema Nicole was and if she was like me and if she even knew who I was. I held on to my daughter's picture until I drifted off into a drunken slumber.

G STREET CHRONICLES
A LITERARY POWERHOUSE
WWW.GSTREETCHRONICLES.COM

Chapter Four

Pinky
Grudges

It's raining outside. I hate when it rains. Every time it rains, my old battle wounds ache. I haven't been the same since someone cut the brake line on my Ducati on that fateful night many moons ago. I was lucky I was able to walk away with my life back then. I guess I could take a few aches and pains here and there now since my life had been spared. The doctors called my survival and recovery nothing short of a miracle. Since the day I woke up in the wee hours of the morning with all kinds of tubes and IVs coming out of every available spot on my body, I haven't been quite right.

Seventeen Years Earlier

When I first opened my eyes, the first thing I noticed was that my body was bandaged from head to toe. The next thing I noticed was the officer who was looking at me like I was the second coming of Jesus Christ himself. She wasn't dressed like a cop, but I surely recognized that badge swinging from her neck. I knew if she was in plain clothes that she was most likely a detective and that couldn't have been a good sign. Detectives only show up when some serious shit happened; and as far as I could remember, I had been involved in plenty of serious shit. My mind wasn't that cloudy.

I tried to speak to the officer and ask her how I had gotten there, but the thick plastic tube that was lodged down my throat wouldn't allow me to talk. I watched the young officer rush out of the room; I wanted to call after her and beg her not to leave me alone. I had never been fond of the police considering the line I work I was in, but anyone who could tell me how I had gotten there was a friend of mine.

Moments after the young woman left my room, she returned with what looked like every available nurse and doctor on the ward that was on duty that morning. The doctors and nurses immediately started asking me how I felt and if I knew where I was. All I could do was nod my head up and down as they worked to remove the tubing from my throat.

Once they removed the hard plastic that was restricting me from talking, I tried to sit up. That's when the pain shot through every nook and cranny of my body. I fell back on the bed wincing in pain when my body hit the firm hospital mattress. The nurses were all busying themselves with checking my vitals. The doctor, along with the police officer, approached my bedside. Once the nurses were finished doing whatever they were doing, they left us alone.

I was still nervous to have a police officer that close to me. After all, I had tried to kill Dread and I knew that he was still alive. For all I knew, the police were there to lock me up for attempted murder. I had never thought twice about taking someone's life. It was never personal. It was always business. This was the first time I had tried to kill someone on a personal level and I felt like trying to kill Dread may have backfired on me.

I lay there in the bed waiting for the officer to slap cuffs on me; but instead, she took out a notepad and the doctor began asking me a series of questions.

"Ms. York, do you know where you are? You don't have to speak if you can't just yet. Just nod or shake your head to respond."

I cleared my throat and tried to speak. My throat was scratchy from the foreign object that had been lodged down my esophagus for God only knew how long.

"I know I'm in a hospital," I managed to croak.

"Good. Well Ms. York, my name is Doctor Gandy. You are in G.W. Hospital. You took a nasty spill on your bike a few weeks back. I must say it's amazing that you're alive. You've been under my care and in a

drug-induced coma for two weeks. It was touch and go there for a while, but I think after some vigorous physical therapy, you should be able to return to a pretty normal life. That's the good news. The bad news is that you are going to be here with us for a little while longer. You have quite a bit of healing to do before we are able to release you.

You've broken both of your legs, you have managed to sprain your right wrist, you've ruptured a disk in your back and you have a fractured collarbone. Those things can all be fixed and they are well on their way to healing. I do have to tell you, Ms. York, that you suffered some swelling of the brain and a concussion. So, you're going to have to take it easy and we will have to monitor you until the swelling goes down. I can't say it enough, Ms. York; you're one lucky woman. You will have some scars and you might experience migraines from time to time, but other than that, you should heal in time."

I sat there looking from Doctor Gandy to the officer trying to process everything. Once the doctor finished all he had to say, he excused himself leaving me there with the officer that I would rather not be around right now. The officer offered me a warm smile, but I still wasn't sure if she was there to bust my ass for trying to kill Dread or not, so I played it cool and watched her like a hawk.

She pulled up a chair right next to my bed and looked at her watch and jotted something on that notepad she was still holding.

"Ms. York, my name is Officer Singleton. Do you know why I'm here?"

I had been up for all of seven minutes and I was already sick of being asked that question. Obviously, I didn't know and I wished she would just say whatever she needed to say. The anticipation was killing me. I shook my head back and forth and waited for her to tell me why she was there.

"Ms. York, you were involved in a nearly fatal crash. After we investigated the scene and what was left of your bike, we were able to determine that the brake line on the bike you were operating had been tampered with," she paused to give me time to let it all sink in.

I don't know what kind of reaction she was expecting from me, but I'm sure she wasn't expecting me to smile at her. I already knew this had something to do with Dread. Since the day I shot him, I had been having nothing but bad luck. I missed my mark and he had most likely sent someone to kill me. I was secretly mad at myself for making my hit on Dread personal. I knew better. When you make shit personal, it never goes right. My beef with Dread was definitely personal. He had killed my sister and as soon as I could get out of this hospital, I was going to hunt him down and kill him the way he had done my baby sister the night of my birthday party.

"Is there someone who may want to see you hurt?"

Officer Singleton continued.

I wanted to tell her, "Sure there are tons of people who want to see me hurt and even more people who would rather see me dead," but I wasn't going to say anything else to her. I felt better knowing she wasn't there because the police knew I tried to kill Dread's sorry ass and missed. Instead, they were there because he had probably tried to kill me. Talk about the irony of it all. Then it hit me. Where was Neko? I was headed to see him and that's the last thing I remembered before waking up here.

"Officer Singleton...were you able to reach my ahh...boyfriend? His name is Neko Reynolds," I managed to ask, even though my throat felt like the Sahara Desert.

She looked at me and smiled weakly. "Ms. York, that is another thing I am here to talk to you about. Two men have inquired about you, but..." then her voice trailed off.

"But what?"

"Ms. York, I don't know exactly how to say it but... for your protection we told anyone that inquired about you, that you didn't make it. We didn't have a next of kin to contact and we didn't know who made the attempt on your life. We felt it was in your best interest to keep you away from anyone who could have posed a threat. You have had one attempt on your life. We didn't want anyone to make another one and succeed at it this time."

I sat there listening to this woman tell me that I was dead to anyone who would even bother to look for me.

"Why would you tell him that?" I screamed and thrashed about the hospital bed. Although it hurt to move, I wanted to get out of there and I wanted to leave now. I had to get to Neko. I had to let him know I wasn't dead. We had just made things right between us.

Detective Singleton quickly pushed the call button and the nurses filed in one by one. They surrounded the bed where I was still trying to get up so I could be with Neko. One male nurse held me down while another injected some clear liquid into my arm. Instantly, I felt like I couldn't move. Whatever the liquid was that she injected into my arm had a quick effect. I tried to concentrate on fighting them off of me. I wanted answers for their actions.

The last thing I remembered was thinking why hadn't Neko come for me? If he really loved me like he said he did, he would have demanded that he see me.

My eyes fluttered closed and everything faded to black.

Present Day…

I never got quite right like that stupid Doctor Gandy

said I would. I was far from right in my opinion. Once they let me out of that hospital, things never seemed to be the same. I wasn't interested in anything but surviving. I couldn't go back to dancing and that was one of the only things I was good at besides being a killer. My body was scarred from the attempt on my life. I didn't dare get naked in front of anyone for money again. I found a bullshit job on campus at Howard University. All I could do was go totally legit. With my body all scarred up, I could never dance again; and I don't know too many people who would hire a hit woman who had missed her own personal mark, so I left that career choice behind as well.

Now all I have left in my life are scars, a huge chip on my shoulder and an insatiable thirst for revenge if the opportunity ever presents itself. Although I'm doubtful that I will ever run across Dread again...if I do, I will jump at the chance to rock his dome. All of my downfalls and everything I lost is because of him and if I see him, I won't hesitate to shoot on sight. I wouldn't give a damn if it were on a busy street; I would kill him...and this time, I would not miss my mark.

Chapter Five

Neko
Something Ain't Right

My wife Rhina and I watched as YaSheema Nicole packed up the last of her things. I couldn't believe that in the morning, she was going to head to the one place I didn't want her to go. Although I had forbid her to go to Washington, D.C., she had applied to attend Howard University and had been accepted. I had secretly wished that they would have rejected her application so she wouldn't go. I wanted the best for YaSheema Nicole, and that included a great education which was something my sisters and I never cared to get; we were raised to survive by way of our father's methods of getting' money; that is until tragedy struck and scared us straight. Well, it scared me straight.

I was extremely excited to know I had raised my niece right and that she wanted to go to school; but I wanted her to do it closer to home and definitely not in D.C. After losing everyone I loved, there was no way

I wanted her to start digging and have the darkness I tried to shield her from come out to rear its ugly head. I had tried my best to tell her as little as possible about her mother and her father and our notorious bloodline; but the more I tried to keep it under wraps, the more she inquired.

When she was a little girl and first started asking questions about her parents, I had gone as far as telling her that they had both been killed in a car accident and were in heaven. That lasted until she was about twelve years old. Then she had been cleaning out the basement with her Aunt Rhina and came across old newspaper clippings of her mother's death along with the only information I had on her punk ass daddy Dread. After YaSheema Nicole got an eyeful of the truth about her parents, she was hell bent on finding her father, claiming that she didn't feel adequate and that finding him would complete her. No matter how much I tried to deter her from knowing the truth...the harder she pushed to find it.

For two years after she found those old clippings, I had grown weary of trying to hide the truth from her. I finally caved in and told YaSheema Nicole that her father was alive; or at least that the last time I had checked he was alive. I secretly hoped the stupid muthafucka' was dead. I told her just enough to keep her at bay. The little information I had given her seemed to keep her satisfied for a while; but not more than a month later, she was asking me all kinds of wild shit about her parents.

Rhina tried to get me to tell YaSheema Nicole the truth, but she hadn't lived the nightmare like I had. She didn't know how detrimental my telling my niece about her past could be. Rhina thought the more YaSheema knew, the more likely she would be to just leave it alone. Obviously she didn't know our niece. Rhina didn't know the whole story behind why I had taken my niece and ran, and I never had any intention on telling either of them shit. The less they knew, the better off they would be.

It was about a year after that when I started to notice a serious change in YaSheema; a change that scared the shit out of me. I had caught her talking to herself. I didn't say anything the first time I had caught her looking as though she were having an argument with herself. She was seated in the family room supposedly watching TV when she started screaming *shut up* to someone who wasn't there. I stood off to the side and watched my niece in horror as she yelled, cursed and screamed. She had a wild look on her face and it made my stomach turn. I had seen that face before. It had been many years ago. It was the same wild look her mother—my sister NiQue gave me the night she had come to kill us both.

I eased into the room and when YaSheema finally looked up and saw me, she settled down like nothing had happened. She was her normal calm chipper self. I think that was the part that scared me the most. Her mother was the same way. She was calm one minute and the next she was full blown out of control. When I questioned YaSheema on what happened, she claimed she was caught up in the movie she was watching. I wasn't buying it because I knew there was nothing on that television that would have caused the outburst I had seen. The local news was depressing, but it should not have caused her to go off the deep end.

The very next time I caught her lunchin' out was right after an extremely heated argument she had with my wife Rhina. After Rhina and YaSheema Nicole exchanged some unpleasant words, YaSheema Nicole ran off to her room, slamming her door behind her. When I climbed the spiral stairs to try to diffuse the situation, I could hear her talking to someone. It wasn't her talking that made me stop dead in my tracks. It was what she said that made my blood run cold as the North Pole.

"I hate that nosy ole' bitch and if you don't make her mind her fuckin' business, I'm gonna' wind up getting angry and you don't want me to do that; do you?"

"Takiya, just chill. She's just doing what parents do. There ain't no need to take shit to another level."

"Humpf! You might want to control that loose booty, big mouth slut then; because if she pops off like that again, ain't no telling what I'll do to her. And for the record...she ain't our mother. Our mother is dead and she is probably the reason why. She got

you and Uncle Neko wrapped around her finger, but not me! I know she's the reason Uncle Neko won't tell us what we need to know. We need to get at her ass and get her out of the way. Then maybe Unc will ease up on us without his loud-mouthed wife always barging in."

"She really ain't that bad Takiya. You gotta give her a chance. Besides, how do you expect her to act with you wildin' out every chance you get."

I heard the conversation from the other side of the bedroom door. I knew I was hearing my niece's voice on both sides of the conversation, but it was like she was changing her voice. One minute it was YaSheema Nicole's voice and then all the replies were her voice too, but the tone was sinister. It made shivers run down my spine.

I had seen and heard some ill shit dealing with my sisters and something about hearing my niece talk to herself took me to the night I saved her from being murdered by her own mother. It was so eerily familiar. I didn't want to open the door because I was afraid of what I would find on the other side of it. My hands trembled when I turned the knob. Once I opened the door, my eyes darted all around the room hoping that the wicked conversation that had taken place was between my niece and one of her friends. When my eyes landed on YaSheema, she was seated at her desk in front of her computer and she was all alone.

"Who were you talking to?" I asked nervously.

She whipped her head around and looked surprised to see me standing there. "Oh, I was having a webcam chat with one of my friends from school. Why?" she asked me curiously.

"I just thought I heard something I didn't want to hear. So, who did you say you were talking to again?" I asked, stepping further into her room. I was careful to leave the door open... just in case. I had noticed some strange behavior from her in the past, and I knew very well who her mother was and how troubled she had been before she died. I didn't put anything past anyone who shared the same DNA as me. We were all screwed up and suspect of having severe issues.

"Oh, I was talking to Cassandra from my English lit class," she said nonchalantly.

I knew she wasn't telling the truth. There was no way she was able to make it from arguing downstairs to her room and chatting with anyone in that small amount of time. I started to press the issue; but I have to admit, I was shook and didn't want to know any more. The truth might have made me keep a promise I had made to myself many years earlier. I had said that if my niece ever showed signs of being anything like my sister, I would drop her ass off at a mental hospital and never look back. Instead, I backed out of her room slowly. YaSheema turned her back to me and faced her computer.

I stood there looking at the young woman I had raised and my love for her made me soften up a bit.

Maybe she was telling me the truth. She was in front of her computer and she had never lied to me before so why would she start now?

"Look, if you ever need to talk, YaSheema...you know your Aunt Rhina and I are here for you."

Then I turned to leave. Before I could get a few paces away from the door, she called after me.

"Uncle Neko."

I stopped and turned around thinking maybe she was going to open up about what I had heard and her peculiar behavior. Instead, she kept her back to me.

"Next time knock," she said coldly.

I started to reprimand her for demanding that I knock on a door that I paid for, but something in her voice told me that might not be such a good idea after all. Instead, I closed her door and let her be. I didn't think I could face what I thought was happening.

That was several years ago and I hadn't seen or heard her act like that since that day and I was grateful she hadn't given me any more reasons to think of dropping her off at an asylum; because if I had to, I would.

CHAPTER SIX

YaSheema Nicole
On The Midnight Train From Georgia

I had made plans to go out with my girl Cassandra from Bankhead. We went to school together and she was one of my only friends. Honestly, she was the only person I could connect with. Anyone else that I seemed to try and befriend, Takiya had a problem with. Cassandra was the only one Takiya seemed to like and I was glad she allowed me to have at least one friend. I think Takiya only let me keep Cassandra around because she was never any real threat to us. It was bad enough I didn't know who I really was or where I had come from. So it felt good to have one friend outside of Takiya who I was able to connect with.

I started getting ready to go out. Cassandra and I had planned to hit up as many clubs as we could. It was our last night together and we wanted to go out with a bang. She was going to attend Spelman, and since I was going to Howard we planned to live it up our last night together until I came home for winter break.

I beat my face with just a little eyeliner and eye shadow to match my blue tube dress that I had to practically beg Uncle Neko to let me get. I knew he couldn't tell me no about the dress. I had been a straight A student and I had never been too much of a problem besides the shit Takiya got me into from time to time, which was nothing that had ever landed me in any real hot water. The only issues he had with the dress was that he thought it was too much for me. It took me two weeks and me being extra nice to Aunt Rhina before he finally agreed to let me have it.

By nine o'clock, I had scooped Cassandra and her friend Vernita up and we were waiting in line at Club Inferno. We could hear the music pulsating through the speakers while we waited on the outside in the line to get in.

I was chatting with Cassandra when a group of guys walked right past the line of angry waiting patrons and dapped up the security guards who quickly removed the ropes and let the guys inside.

"Do you see that shit? He's just gonna' let them waltz right in like he doesn't see us standing here," Cassandra said fussing. She got out of her spot in the line and headed straight to where the bouncers were standing like they hadn't done anything underhanded. By the way Cassandra's nostrils were flared and the way her neck was rolling from side to side as she talked, I knew she was giving the overweight bouncer a piece of her mind. I left my place in line, leaving Vernita standing there. I could tell as I approached that from the looks of things, the bouncer was not happy about being told how to do his job by a feisty female.

"How the fuck are you gonna let them go in ahead of us like we aren't standing here?" Cassandra said, swinging her hair and pointing her long manicured finger in the bouncer's face.

"Look, lil' mama. I suggest you get your lil' hot ass in line and wait your turn like everyone else," the bouncer said, laughing at Cassandra like she was a joke.

"Hot ass? I know you ain't gonna just disrespect me like that! Oh, I get it. You're a faggot. You'd rather have a club full of sweaty men," Cassandra shot back. I tugged at her arm and tried to pull her away. If she kept this up...we'd never get in.

"Come on girl. Your arguing with him ain't gonna get us up in there any faster," I said, trying my best to talk her down. I knew my friend very well and she was not one to back down from anything. If she had a point to prove, she would go through the fires of hell to prove it.

"Nah. Fuck that. He's just being a butt munching faggot. He knows what he did wasn't right. Just because no one else is gonna call him on his bullshit doesn't mean I ain't," Cassandra said, pulling away from me and crossing her arms over her heaving chest. She planted her feet firmly in their spot and she wouldn't move. She was determined to cause as much of a commotion as she possibly could.

"You better listen to your bitch because she's got the right idea...to wait like everybody else. So take your ass back over there and get in line before someone takes your spot and you watch the show from the sidewalk," the bouncer said, clearly annoyed with Cassandra's slick tongue.

I had tried to handle things like a lady. I tried to be civilized, but this dude was asking for it. I knew if he kept up his tough guy act Takiya would surely start to stir and that was something none of us needed. Takiya turnt up was a bad situation.

Did this nigga call us a bitch?

Oh shit. It was too late. Takiya heard him and she was no doubt ready to blow. There was no way I could try and talk her down now. Even if I could, I would look crazy standing there talking to myself. I tried to suppress her, but she was angry. It didn't take much to rile her up and now was no exception to her rules.

"Nigga, who you calling a bitch?"

It just slipped from my lips. I didn't mean for it to. Takiya was in full effect and the more audience she had, the better. She was about to show her ass and she didn't care who saw it. I wanted to turn around and run away, but my legs felt like weights were holding me down. I felt cold and then it felt like my temperature shot up twenty degrees. Explaining the rage Takiya was feeling over this man calling her a bitch was indescribable. I hated when she got mad.

"I don't see your momma with her shriveled up pussy out here, so you must have me mistaken for another bitch. Nigga, you ain't nothin' but a fudge packin' undercover homo. That's why you let those dudes in without a blink of an eye. See, I know your type. You're just a sissy ass muthafucka' pretending to be all hard by working at this pissy ass club. You only work here to play straight. I've seen your kind before. I can see that shit all over your face. You know what? You and your lil' faggity friends can have this muthafucka'! I ain't trippin off of this club," Takiya said.

She was furious and it really wasn't that serious. There were a million clubs in Atlanta. We could easily go to any one of them. I didn't need any drama. I was supposed to be partying the night away; not involved in an argument that really wasn't worth it.

Vernita stood there with her mouth wide open. Even Cassandra stopped and gawked at *us*. I don't think anyone was expecting things to escalate like they were.

"I think maybe we should just find another club to go to ya'll," Vernita said, trying to diffuse the time bomb named Takiya who was now in full show out mode.

"Yeah, maybe we should leave," Takiya sneered.

Cassandra didn't say another word. She was so in awe of *our* behavior that she didn't put up any more resistance. Vernita looked relieved that we were trying to be sensible and walk away like ladies. What Vernita didn't know was that Takiya was mad and she wasn't done with the bouncer. Not by a long shot. Vernita and I started to walk away when Takiya had to have the last word.

"I hope you know this shit ain't over, nigga. I'll be seeing you soon and I'ma make you eat your words! You can bet that," Takiya said with clenched teeth and her fist balled up so tight I could feel her digging her nails into the palms of our hands.

Cassandra pulled me away from the bouncer and led me back to the car. We all got in and I felt everything happening in reverse. The weights I felt from before felt like they were being lifted. I felt like I could move. I wasn't being guided and played with like the puppet Takiya thought I was.

I knew she was close by and she was still very angry. I knew damn well she wasn't going to give up that easy. Surprisingly though, she didn't surface anymore that night, Vernita suggested we hit another spot called the G Street Bar and Grill in Stockbridge. I had never been there, but I was willing to go anywhere as long as it kept Takiya from making a scene. This was my last night in the A. I just wanted to enjoy it.

We pulled into the bar and the tension in the car was so thick you needed a machete to cut it. We drove all the way over to Stockbridge in silence. Every now and again, I could feel Cassandra watching me. I know she was curious about my behavior. I had never tripped out like that before around her, so I knew she was shocked by what had gone down. I had always remained calm and level headed unless Takiya showed up to pull her lil' strings. Little did I know, Takiya's puppeteer show had only just begun.

Chapter Seven

Mission Impossible
Pinky York

I hate this 9-5 grinding shit. I was sitting in my office going through the new student admissions and assigning the faculty their security badges. I knew I had better finish placing the students in their respective living quarters before my boss had a fit. He was already on my ass for not having each student assigned to their rooms yet. I promised him that I would have them completed by the end of business today. I knew I was nowhere near finished and it would take a miracle for me to get them done. Since it was Friday and it was nice outside, my mind was on going for a ride on my bike.

To tell you the truth, I just didn't feel like doing anything that had anything to do with work. I'm not the working girl type. I am used to making my own money and working for no one but myself. Having someone give me orders and fetch their coffee makes me want to put a gun to my boss' head and making my gun bang. Now that's some shit I'm used to. That's all I have ever really been good at. Well that and shaking my ass. However, that life is over. Or so I thought. I sifted through the pile of housing requests and that's when I couldn't believe whose name was on my housing list. I had to blink to make sure my eyes weren't playing tricks on me.

I know damn well I can't be holding the form for Ms. YaSheema Nicole Evans. I read further down the form almost afraid that it really was who I thought it was. I mean really...how many people named their children YaSheema? I only knew two of them and they were both a part of the family who formerly employed me as their cleanup woman. There was YaSheema Clayton who I knew was dead and I was there the day my boss' daughter was laid to rest. I knew it couldn't have been *that* YaSheema. The only YaSheema I knew of outside of YaYa Clayton was her niece, which was Dread's daughter that he had with that crazy bitch NiQue. As far as I was concerned, the whole family was grimy. Even the extended members of the Reynolds-Clayton clan were out of control. I wasn't one to talk because I had done more than enough of my fair share of dirt, but that family was the worst. They used to keep bodies droppin' left and right and the scandal among them was never ending. I didn't mind it though, because they were good to me even though they were all shifty in their own little way.

I couldn't help but smile. Maybe this bullshit job

had been good for something after all. I inspected the form closely and I confirmed what I had suspected. Under the guardian's name on the form was another name I was very familiar with. My emotions rushed to my head; almost causing another one of these damn headaches the doctors had warned me about years ago. The name brought back so many memories. Neko Reynolds was named as the legal guardian of YaSheema Nicole Evans.

It had been seventeen long years since I had seen or heard from Neko. I thought I had filed my feelings for him in a box labeled, *never again*. Just seeing his name damn near took my breath away. I tried to get my breathing under control and kept reading over the form. Next to Neko's name was another name I wasn't familiar with. It read Doctor Rhina Diaz-Reynolds. She was listed as the other guardian and I felt my heart shatter. Neko had moved on. From the form I was looking at, he had gotten married and he apparently had forgotten all about me.

I slammed the papers on the desk and tried to hide my hurt and frustration. I was upset with him for moving on. He never even bothered to confirm if I was dead or alive before he picked up the next bitch.

I don't even know why I was so upset. Had the shoe been on the other foot, I would have bailed on him too. Not to mention, I hadn't been exactly up front and honest with Neko during our relationship. I was juggling two men at once. I had slept with Dread and

I had even gotten pregnant and didn't know if Neko or Head was the father. I guess I really shouldn't be mad that Neko moved on. For all he knew, I really was dead. Those bitch ass cops took care of that years ago. They said it was to protect me, but it didn't do anything but take away the last miniscule piece of life I had.

Now I was here processing paperwork for future students of Howard University when my name should have been the one on the line next to Neko's as his wife. I stamped YaSheema Nicole's application and approved her dorm request and tried to finish the rest of my day without thinking about the *what ifs*.

What if none of that shit had happened? Would Neko and I have been married? Would we have children? I almost broke down thinking of what my life could have been. I honestly felt like losing Neko was karma kicking me in the ass. After all...I killed a baby that could have been our child. I guess God punished me in other ways. He took the only man I had ever loved. That was nothing more than payback for all the underhanded things I had done in my past. My past wasn't exactly clean and I had to settle my debt I owed to the Devil at some point. Losing the man I loved and having to live with the memory of lying on that table in the abortion clinic killing my own baby was definitely torture. I was heartless and cruel when I was paid to be that way, but nothing could compare to me taking the life of my unborn child.

I pushed away from my desk and got up. I gathered

my things and prepared the lie I was about to tell my boss about why I had to leave early. There was no way I would be able to finish the rest of my day like this.

I made a copy of YaSheema Evans' file, replaced the original and then headed to my supervisor's office. I made up some shit about not feeling well. I didn't care if he believed me or not. I had too many things on my mind and being cooped up in this office wasn't helping. I knew what would help though and I was going to make sure I did everything I could to close up all loose ends I had with the Reynolds', Clayton's, and Evans' families. If I didn't close those doors, then I would forever be caught up in this world wind of confusion. It was beyond time for me to take my life back. I didn't want to be stuck wondering how things could have been. I was going to find out if Neko ever really loved me. I had to know for my own sanity. I wasn't going to call him either. I was going to take a trip to the A. The conversation we needed to have had to be done face to face. There was no other way. Then I was going to find Dread. He and I still had unfinished business. I learned long ago that you never left a target alive. Dread was out there somewhere and I had let him live far too long. He took the only person I ever loved and for that he was definitely going to pay. He killed my sister and I hadn't forgotten about that shit. He took the only person who loved me wholeheartedly.

I walked out of my office and to the garage. I put my pink helmet on and hopped on my pink bike. It was the only piece of my past that I had left. It was the last thing Neko gave me before we fell out and then he was told by those punk cops that I was dead.

The accident never made me fearful of riding my bikes. It was the only thing I had left of who I used to be. I sped out of the garage feeling better than I started out. I guess because I had two missions to complete. I was going to see Neko and get the answers I needed and I was going to find Dread. I had to do it so I could move on. I needed closure on my feelings for Neko and I needed to kill Dread for killing my sister many moons ago. It was definitely time to put an end to the *what ifs* that haunted me.

CHAPTER EIGHT

When Opportunity Knocks
Dread

I hated when I had to do these small time hosting gigs. Crack had talked me into doing these showcases to keep myself afloat. The only reason I did it was to keep Queen and Crack off of my back about me wasting my life. Queen would never be able to understand what I was really feeling. I may have come off as arrogant and secure, but that wasn't the truth. I felt like shit. I had let my life fall apart. My life hadn't been the same since I met YaSheema Clayton and her family and friends.

I can't say I regret meeting YaYa because shawty was official. She should have been my wife. Instead, she was ripped from me and that started the downward spiral in my life. I looked for comfort in the arms of her friend NiQue, who I found out later was her sister.

That whole family was insane. I was so petrified of that family that I abandoned my daughter out of fear of them. There seemed like there was a dark cloud hanging over their family and I didn't want any parts of it. I left my daughter –YaSheema Nicole – with her uncle Neko because I was afraid of what else would happen to me if I stuck around. Nothing but tragedy followed them; and I figured if I steered clear of them, then their curse wouldn't attach itself to me.

I got myself ready to go onstage and host a bogus DMV Hip Hop All-Star banquet. I didn't want to be here. I would rather be in the confines of my house with a big bottle of Ciroc and a pound of Kush. The thought of leaving and going to the nearest liquor store entered my mind. I immediately started thinking of what lie I could tell Queen and Crack for missing the event. Since I knew Queen and Crack had booked this stupid gig, I had better make the best of it. There was no lie I could tell to get out of it, so I had better just do it to keep them off of my ass.

I went through the motions of hosting the banquet, but I couldn't help checking the time after every guest speaker spoke. I wanted to get out of here and catch the liquor store before they closed. The drinks they were serving weren't worth shit. They were watered down and I needed something with some kick to it. When the banquet finally wrapped up, I went back to what was supposed to be my dressing room and prepared to leave. I had fifteen minutes before the liquor stores in the city closed and I intended to get there before they did. There was a knock on my door and Queen walked in before I could say it was ok for her to come in.

"Are you busy?"

"If you mean busy like I'm leaving...then yeah, I'm really busy," I said smugly.

"I have someone I want you to meet before you go," Queen said. I knew she wasn't asking. She was telling me that I had to meet whoever it was she wanted me to meet or I would have to hear about it later. I nodded my head and flopped back down in the metal chair and waited for her to get whoever it was she was excited for me to see. A minute later, she returned with a tall dark skin woman. She was dressed in a black cocktail dress that she filled out to the nines.

"Dread, this is Ms. Grey. She heads up the arts and cultural division at Howard University. She wanted to speak with you about an opportunity she may have for you."

I looked the woman over and couldn't help but notice the way her curves hugged her dress and her smooth dark skin reminded me of Hershey's milk chocolate. At least if I was going to miss the liquor store, Ms. Grey was nice to look at.

"Nice to meet you, Mr. Evans; I'm a huge fan of your music," Ms. Grey said, extending her hand to me. I nodded in her direction, dismissing her gesture and wished I could hurry her up so I could get out of there.

"I won't take up too much of your time, but I head up the arts program at Howard and I wanted to know if you would be interested in doing a few lectures at the university on the history of DMV music?" Ms. Grey said, smiling.

I don't know what I thought she was going to ask me, but I sure didn't think it was going to be this. What did I know about lecturing some kids on music? At the height of my music career everything I had was stripped from me because I couldn't keep my dick in my pants. The only thing I was capable of teaching them was what not to do in the music industry. That shit didn't even require more than one lecture. I would be able to wrap up all my lessons in one sentence: *Leave women alone.*

"If you don't mind me asking, Ms. Grey...what's the catch? I'm sure you know I haven't done anything in regards to music in about seventeen years and I don't plan on starting now. Hell, the only reason I'm here tonight is because she made me," I said, sarcastically pointing at Queen.

Queen screwed up her face and I knew I had better be nice to Ms. Grey or I would have to hear about my behavior later.

"There's no catch, Mr. Evans. There are classes and lectures being held all over the country like the one we have developed. 9th Wonder teaches a class at N.C. Central University. McNally Smith College in Minnesota offers a full course where you can get a degree in Hip-Hop. Berklee College of Music has a Business of Hip-Hop/Urban Music Symposium. It has been done, Mr. Evans, and I think with your help, we could bring it to

Howard University. I am sure you know we have had several artists grace our hallways and we would like to have you come on board as one of the instructors. We could get any one of our celebrity alum to do this, but we want you," Ms. Grey said, smiling.

I don't know if she thought I was a fool, but no one would take something like this serious. If they did take it serious, where was Puff Daddy and why hadn't they offered him this opportunity? He was a better candidate than I was. At least the man attended Howard. I was a has been doing bullshit gigs to make ends meet. This lady was pulling my leg and if it wasn't for Queen standing there breathing down my neck, I would have told Ms. Grey to fuck off. I didn't care how fine she was.

"Ms. Grey, I ain't sure you want me to do this. I don't know what I could possibly teach these kids," I said, hoping she would see that I wasn't in the mood for the bullshit.

Queen didn't look pleased that I was blowing Ms. Grey off and I didn't really care. I only had ten minutes before I could find a liquor store and they were both holding me up from doing so.

"I hope you will reconsider, Mr. Evans. I think you are just what we need to pull this off. If you change your mind, here's my business card. Call me and we can discuss this in further detail," Ms. Grey said, handing me her business card.

I politely took her card and stuffed it in my back

pocket and excused myself. I left both Ms. Grey and Queen standing there. I knew this wasn't going to be the last time I heard about this "supposed" opportunity; but before I had to hear about it again, I was going to be high and drunk when Queen and Crack came my way to badger me about it again.

CHAPTER NINE

YaYa Nicole
Believe

I woke up with a pounding headache. It must have been the drinks from last night that had my temples rocking.

"I think you should get up and change your clothes," Takiya whispered in my ear.

I ignored her and rolled over and looked at the clock on my nightstand. It only read 7:00 a.m. and we weren't pulling out to leave for D.C. until noon.

"Leave me alone. I still got some time to sleep," I groaned and pulled the covers over my head and ignored Takiya and her ruckus.

"If you don't get your ass up out of that bed and get out of those clothes, you ain't gonna' have nothing but time. You're gonna have all the time in the world. You'll be sitting in a jail cell with nothing but time on your hands. I don't think you have it in you to waste away for twenty-five to life," Takiya chuckled.

I sat up because clearly Takiya wasn't going to let

me sleep until we had to make the nine-hour trip to D.C.

"What are you talking about? I ain't in the mood for your lil' rhymes and games," I said, annoyed with her. She had showed out last night and I wasn't feeling her right now.

"Take a look in the mirror, sleeping beauty," she giggled hysterically in my ear.

I swung my legs over the side of the bed and decided to humor her. Besides, if I didn't, she would never let me get a few more hours' worth of sleep in and for some reason I was drained. I honestly didn't know why I felt like I had been through a war. I got a glimpse of myself in my mirror and had to stifle my screams. My entire body – my blue dress included – was covered in what looked like blood. Even my hair was a sickening hue of brownish-red.

"See I told you," Takiya laughed hysterically.

"What the fuck did you do?" I started to peel the clothes away from my body afraid of what I would find when I got them off. As soon as I was completely naked, I scanned my body from head to toe to see where the blood could have come from. I even stuck my hand between my legs to make sure I hadn't come on my period, even though there was way too much blood all over my body for me to be my period.

Takiya was still laughing as if I had told her the funniest joke she'd ever heard. "Calm down bitch. It ain't your blood."

"Well, whose is it then?" I stood there naked and trembling, waiting for Takiya to give me some type of explanation on why I would be covered in someone else's blood.

"Aww, you shouldn't worry about that. The less you know, the better off you'll be."

"I don't know what kind of game you're playing, but I don't want to play anymore. Takiya, this shit ain't funny. Either tell me whose blood this is, or I'm gonna tell Uncle Neko and Aunt Rhina. You know what'll happen if they find out about this don't you? They'll put us both away. Do you want that?"

"You ain't gonna tell either of them old fools nothin'," Takiya snorted.

"Glad you think I won't. Just because you don't trust them doesn't mean I don't," I said, stepping over the pile of bloody clothes and grabbing my bathrobe off of the back of my bedroom door. I had every intention of going straight to Uncle Neko and Aunt Rhina. I had the sinking feeling something pretty fucked up happened for me to be covered in that amount of blood.

"Wait! I'll tell you if you swear you'll just leave it alone."

"I can't make that kind of promise, Takiya. You know I can't!"

"Well, if you can't promise me that this will stay between you and me, then I can't tell you shit. When you run off to tell your uncle and his bitch then you will look like a fool because you won't even know what you are telling them. The choice is up to you," Takiya said, growing quiet.

I knew she had me between a rock and a hard place. I had to know what happened and the only way she was going to tell me was if I swore not to say anything to Uncle Neko and Aunt Rhina. I weighed my pros and cons and decided after very little thought to promise Takiya I would keep whatever she had done to myself.

"I promise I won't rat you out, Takiya. Now please tell me what happened last night because I don't remember anything," I said sheepishly. I wanted to kick myself for giving in to her so easily, but that was nothing new. I had always given in to her and today was no different.

I swear if you ever tell a soul about this you're gonna regret it," she threatened.

"I swear I won't say anything," I said, desperate to know what she'd done.

Takiya giggled and my blood ran cold in my veins. For some reason, I knew I had just made a deal with Lucifer himself.

"Remember that bitch ass bouncer from last night?"

I nodded my head up and down slowly. "Yeah, I remember him," I said carefully. All of sudden, I remembered the threat Takiya had made the night before to the rude bouncer. She had told him to watch his back and something told me she meant every word of the threat.

"Well, let's just say *we* paid him a visit after you

thought *we* called it a night."

"What do you mean *we* paid him a visit, Takiya? Now is not the time to be vague. What did you do?"

Takiya giggled again and it made my skin crawl.

"I told him he was gonna regret trying to play *us* for a fool. After you dropped Cassandra and Vernita off, *we* left out and waited for the fat fuck to leave the club for the night. When he wobbled his steroid injected ass to his car...*we* shut him up for good. I bet he won't call another woman a bitch. If he does, it will be with pen and paper because he doesn't have lips to call anyone anything anymore."

"What do you mean he doesn't have lips? I'm so confused," I said shivering.

"You can't be that dumb, YaSheema. I cut off his lips and tongue so he can't ever call another woman a bitch again. I left him in the parking lot of the club; and if he's lucky, someone found his bitch ass leaking beside his car where *we* left him."

"What the fuck do you mean *we*? I ain't have nothin' to do with that shit!" I jumped up and stripped out of my blood-stained clothes in a panic. I heard footsteps outside my door. I looked at my arms and upper torso which were covered in brown, dried blood and quickly threw on my robe. I couldn't let Uncle Neko or Aunt Rhina see me like this. They would both surely freak out. As soon as I slid the bathrobe over my body, there was a knock on my bedroom door.

"YaYa, are you up? Breakfast is ready," I heard Aunt

Rhina chirp from the other side of the door.

"I'll be right down," I said, trying my best not to break down. I wanted to fling the door open and confess what Takiya had done; but there was no way that Rhina or Uncle Neko would believe me. Knowing Rhina, she would haul me off to the police station her damn self.

"I think you should just let things be. If you tell either of them anything, it could mean trouble for all of us. You should just let things be the way they are and keep it moving; because if you don't, you will pay the consequences."

I sunk back down on my bed and thought about what Takiya said. I didn't want to take the fall for a crime I didn't remember committing. After thinking on it long and hard, I tried rationalizing things. I couldn't remember doing any of the things Takiya said *we* did. If I couldn't remember doing them, then I was convinced that I hadn't done them. This wasn't the first time that Takiya had tried to sway me to believe something other than the truth. I crept out of my room and tiptoed out down the hallway to the bathroom. I turned the shower on as hot as it would go and got in. I scrubbed my skin raw.

"Just in case," I said out loud. I think I was trying to make myself believe that I hadn't done anything Takiya accused me of doing.

Boy, oh boy, was I wrong.

Chapter Ten

Gone
Neko Reynolds

The day I had been dreading was finally here. It was the day YaSheema was leaving for D.C. No matter how hard I tried to keep her from attending school in the District, the more she protested. I eventually gave in and I'm starting to regret it. My stomach keeps flip flopping and something is telling me I made a huge mistake.

Today was the day I drove my niece to D.C. and dropped her off for college. The thought of leaving her there made me feel queasy. Rhina fixed breakfast and we were waiting for YaSheema to join us before we hit the road. Rhina had even gone through the trouble of packing lunch for us so we didn't have to buy food while we were on the road. I think she knew I was nervous about going home. D.C. held a lot of bad memories for me and I didn't want to revisit any of them.

"Are you ok?" Rhina said in her sexy, thick Latin

accent. The sound of her voice ordinarily made my dick stand to attention, but my mind was in other places. I barely noticed Rhina staring at me.

I snapped out of my thoughts and focused on my wife who was standing in front of me with her hands on her thick hips.

"Neko, are you gonna be alright? You've been real quiet for the past few days and I don't like it."

"Huh? Yeah. I'm fine. I think I might be coming down with something," I responded, hoping I could hide the lie I was trying to feed her.

"I think you're nervous about taking that trip back home. Maybe we should just fly her up North and ship her things to her. I know D.C. harbors a lot of bad memories for you, but maybe her going up there will show her whatever it is that she is looking for. You know...sooner or later, she is gonna go if she is that determined to make her way up there. There is really nothing we can do to stop her, Neko," Rhina said, rubbing my shoulders.

"I know. I just don't want her to..." I stopped myself from finishing my statement. Even Rhina didn't know everything about my family and why I had flown the coop to Atlanta. She knew bits and pieces. I never gave her the full rundown of my family history. I figured the less she knew, the better off we'd all be.

"I don't want her to get caught up in the city life. She ain't built for it. You know we were raised up there. YaSheema is a country girl. I just don't want anyone taking advantage of her up there," I said, trying to disguise my worry with another lie.

"Papi, you're gonna have to let her go. There's nothing you can do about it but pray for her well-being. Just focus on the fact that she is going to school and she wants to make something of herself. Be content that she is making the right decision by going to school. Who knows...this might be a good experience for her. Just think of all of the good things that can come from her going to school, Papi. We get to be all alone. We can do it all over the house and not worry about YaSheema and her friends catching you bending me over the counter in the kitchen and banging my back out," Rhina said, seductively nibbling my ear.

Rhina's long, soft hair tickled my neck and the reaction that I was used to having toward my wife returned. I felt my manhood rise and stand at attention. Rhina knew just what I liked and always gave me what I needed right when I needed it. Her small hands found their way to my crotch and she started massaging my dick right there at the kitchen table.

"See, Papi...our niece going away could be good for all of us," Rhina giggled as she worked her hand up and down my shaft through my pajama pants.

Right when I was ready to take my wife up on her offer to bend her over the counter, we heard YaSheema making her way down the staircase to join us for breakfast. Rhina took a seat at the table with a wide grin across her face while I scooted my chair up to hide my woody from my niece. If YaSheema had caught us in the act, she would have been grossed out. She never liked seeing Rhina and I affectionate with one another; so her catching us in the act would've driven her crazy.

I sipped my coffee and tried to pretend that I wasn't about to fuck my wife right there in the kitchen when YaSheema walked in. When I looked up at YaSheema, she seemed somewhat vacant. She wasn't acting like today was her big day to move out on her own. She took a seat at the kitchen table and just sat there.

"Well, good morning to you too," I said sarcastically. YaSheema didn't seem to think my joke was funny. She didn't even crack a smile. Instead, she raised her eyebrow in my direction and then pushed her eggs around her plate. Rhina must've picked up on YaSheema's behavior too because she gave me a disapproving look.

"Is everything alright, YaSheema? You don't seem like you're well," Rhina said to her.

"I'm fine. I think maybe I'm nervous about the move," YaSheema responded, pushing her eggs in circles.

YaSheema had a spaced-out look on her face. She was there physically, but I could tell something was troubling her internally. "You know it ain't too late to stay here in Georgia for college. There are plenty of good schools down here that you can attend. With the kind of grades you have, it should be no problem transferring to one of the schools here," I said, making one last ditch attempt to keep my niece close to me.

"Damn, Uncle Neko! How many times do we have to go through the same thing? I'm going to Howard in D.C. and there's nothing you or anyone else can do to stop me," YaSheema said, rolling her grey eyes that mirrored my own and sucking her teeth. Then she glared in Rhina's direction. Over the past few months, she had gotten real comfortable with talking to me in an aggressive manner and I was getting tired of her mouth.

"I think you should watch your mouth, YaSheema Nicole. I ain't one of your lil' friends; the last time I checked, I was frontin' the whole bill for your education and you ain't gonna sit here and disrespect me," I said, taking my stance. I had to put my foot down because she was getting carried away.

"I know who paid the bill. You've reminded me at least ten times in the last twenty-four hours. How could I forget?" she shot back.

"You know you act just like..." I stopped mid-sentence. I knew I was about to say something I was about to regret and since we were on the verge of taking a nine-hour drive back into the last place on Earth that I wanted to be, I figured I had better chill and refrain from telling YaSheema that she was acting like her crazy ass mother.

"I act like who, Uncle Neko? Who do I act like? Is it

my mother you refuse to tell me anything about? Or is it my father that you never mention without cringing? Which one is it?" YaSheema shot back. Her voice was raspy and serious. Her eyes bore holes in me and I just couldn't take the tension and I damn sure wasn't about to get into the same argument that we always got into about her parents. Instead, I pushed away from the kitchen table and walked out before things escalated any further. I was already on the verge of telling her some shit she shouldn't know. I almost told her the truth she had been searching for. I headed up the stairs and I heard Rhina trying to calm YaSheema down.

"I ain't driving to D.C. with him acting like that. I can take the trip on my own! I'm eighteen and I am more than capable of making the journey by myself," YaSheema said, still ranting.

"You know your uncle and I love you very much, YaSheema. We're just trying to protect you; that's all," Rhina said, trying to diffuse the situation.

"Protect me from what? How am I supposed to know what to look out for if ya'll won't tell me anything? You two keep treating me like I'm fragile."

"I think maybe the two of us should take that trip to D.C. together. I think your uncle needs some time to cool down. He's taking it hard that you're leaving. You're the only baby we have and now you're all grown up. It's hard for him to let you go. I know you won't believe this, but it's going to be hard for me to let you go too," Rhina said sincerely.

"But don't you have to work?" I heard YaSheema ask Rhina. I knew she wasn't her aunt's biggest fan, so I knew she would be against riding nine hours up I-85 with her. I felt dirty listening in on their private conversation, but Rhina was saying everything I felt. I wanted to protect *my* YaSheema. She didn't know what kind of world I'd rescued her from, but I guess it was time for me to let her go and do her own thing. I had to find myself and now it was her turn to do the same.

"That's the good thing about having your own practice. You get to call the shots. So...how about it? I could drive you to D.C. and take a flight back in your uncle's place," Rhina offered.

"I don't think Uncle Neko will let you take me. He's already bent out of shape over me going. You taking me to school would be the icing on the cake," YaSheema said to Rhina, finally calming herself down.

"Let me worry about that. Besides, I got people in D.C. That's where I was born and raised and I ain't been back since me and Neko relocated here. Let me make a few phone calls to get someone to cover my patients while we're away and throw a few things in my bags and we can be on the road by noon. How's that sound?" Rhina bargained with YaSheema.

"I guess so. I just don't want Unc mad with me," I heard YaSheema mumble. I couldn't see her face, but her voice spoke volumes. It was time for me to let her go. I heard Rhina making her way out of the kitchen and I took the steps two at a time to avoid being caught eavesdropping. I made it to the bedroom in enough time to flop down on the bed and pretend I hadn't been listening in on their conversation right as Rhina made it to our room. Rhina eased her way over to where I was sitting and sat down next to me.

"Papi, I think we need to talk," Rhina said, looking me in my eyes. I loved this woman. Rhina was the only woman who could make me put up my playa's card. She had been there for me when I was at my lowest point. I loved her for always taking on my burdens and responsibilities and making them her own. She was tender and loving and that was something I had never felt before. I had been in love only one time before Rhina and that was with Pinky, who was long gone.

"Yeah, what do we need to talk about, Rhi?" I asked, knowing fully well what she was going to say, but I couldn't let on that I had heard the entire conversation.

"I think I should take YaSheema to D.C. Before you say no, hear me out please, Papi," Rhina said, rushing her words so I wouldn't interrupt her. "I think it would be good for us both to take the trip together. You, of all people, know we ain't been on the best of terms. Maybe she and I can work on our relationship; you can cool off and she will get to school. What do you say?" Rhina asked, taking my hand.

I looked my beautiful wife –who hadn't aged a bit

since the day we met – in her big, brown eyes and smiled. "Baby, I think you should take her to D.C. It will be good for all of us."

Rhina jumped in my lap and hugged me tight. "Thank you, Papi. I will make sure she's checked in when we get there. I might even stay a couple days. I got family I haven't seen in years. I'm sure they'd be happy to see me too!"

I tried to hide my scowl. I don't know why I gave in so easily. I should have protested or something, but I couldn't. They both seemed so adamant about going, and now Rhina was making a mini-vacation of the whole thing. My stomach started churning and my gut was telling me to put my foot down and demand that neither of them left Georgia; but my heart was soft on both of these women and I couldn't tell them no. I plastered a fake smile on my face and pretended I was happy about releasing the two women I loved the most into the wilds of Drama City without me.

CHAPTER ELEVEN

Dread
Life of Regret

I woke up in the front seat of my car inside of the mini garage of the guest house. Thank God I didn't leave the muthafucka' running or I may have died from carbon monoxide poisoning. I looked around the tiny carport and tried to remember how I had gotten there. The last thing I remembered was catching the liquor store. As soon as I had the bottle of Don Julio in my hands, I popped the cork out and took long gulps of the tequila until my throat burned. Trying to remember how I had gotten home was making my head spin.

I pulled the keys from the ignition and noticed the bottle I purchased the night before was down at my feet and it wasn't completely empty; so I reached down, scooped up the bottle and headed inside. When I got inside, I couldn't think of doing anything better than finishing off the bottle and sleeping clear into the next day. I stumbled through the hallway and into the kitchen and searched for a glass. I couldn't help but laugh at myself when I realized that I hadn't even bothered to wash the dishes. I hunched my shoulders and found a glass on the counter that didn't have cigarette or blunt ashes in it and rinsed it out before I retreated to my room. As soon as I kicked off my pants, there was a knock at my front door. I sucked my teeth and hoped that whoever was on the other side would just go away. I wasn't in the mood for any pep talks or anyone chastising me. I grumbled and opened the door, forgetting that I was only in my boxers. Crack was standing there with a look of disdain written on his face. I guess I would have looked at him funny too if the shoe were on the other foot. I know I was a sight to see standing there in my drawers with a liquor bottle clenched tightly in my hand.

"You care to cover up my nigga and let me in? We need to talk," Crack said with a serious tone in his voice.

I sucked my teeth and moved aside. I knew he wasn't going to leave me alone to enjoy my bottle until I let him say his piece.

"I would have dressed for the occasion if I knew I was having company," I said, trying to lighten the mood. I could see Crack wasn't interested in any of my dry humor and he barely cracked a smile.

"Dunny, I keep telling you your behavior is gonna land the both of us in the dog house with Queen. When I said *I do* to her, I promised myself to never end up there again. She told me about the business opportunity she offered you last night," Crack said, pushing a pile of dirty clothes aside on the worn couch as he took a seat.

"If you came here to talk me into taking that bogus job, you wasted your time, man. That shit ain't for me. You and I both know I don't have no business trying to teach anyone anything about music. My whole career went down the toilet when I got mixed up with some chick and her estranged family members. I don't qualify!" I said, twisting the cap off of the bottle and taking a long gulp from it.

"That's the shit I'm talking about, Dunny. You keep living in the past and it's time for you to move the fuck on. You can't keep making excuses for what happened back then. I ain't saying that shit wasn't crazy; but it's over. It's time to let that shit go. Stop wasting your life away. You ain't got much more time to do shit else with your life. This gig Queen hooked you up with might be your way to put that shit behind you and still do what you love without regret.

You ain't seen your daughter in seventeen years, nigga. You ain't picked up a mic and you ain't dropped no bars on shit in years. You need to get over it and move on. When the shit first happened with NiQue, we left you alone because we couldn't imagine what you were going through losing your girl like that. When you walked away from your daughter, we didn't know you were never gonna look back. We thought you just needed time. Queen and I know we made a mistake letting you just walk away. No real man walks away from their child no matter how fucked up the circumstances are. You might not be able to right all the wrongs my nigga...but you can still live. You ain't gotta die alone in our guesthouse. This shouldn't be your ending. The curtain ain't closed on you yet, Dunny," Crack said. He had never come at me like this about my life.

"I don't know how to make the shit right. If I knew... don't you think I would? I don't even know where to begin," I countered.

"That's bullshit and just another excuse. You got a way to start over and at least work on fixing your life. I ain't asking you no more. I'm telling you to get your shit together or else I can't stand by and watch you kill yourself slowly slurping from a bottle and fucking these nothing ass bitches who don't want shit but a piece of your royalties that don't really amount to shit but a way for you to half ass pay us rent on the guesthouse and stay high and drunk! You're gonna be at Howard U on Monday to teach that seminar, or else I'm gonna have to ask you to get your shit and go," Crack said sternly.

I couldn't believe my boy was leaning on me like this. I knew everything he was saying was true, but I wasn't ready to hear it. I sat down on the chair across from Crack and put my head in my hands.

"I just keep thinking about what if YaYa had never

died. How would my shit have been if she would have gotten that letter to me in time and I had gone to Georgia with her? What if I would have never fucked with NiQue? What if, my nigga? What if?" I asked, trying to keep myself from breaking down.

"You wouldn't have a child out there somewhere. You can't worry about the what ifs now. You can only move on now. Maybe you can right all your wrongs and stop living in regret," Crack said, standing up and walking to the door. He opened the front door and before he walked out, he turned around and looked in my direction one last time. "Queen said the first seminar starts at nine on Monday morning. That should give you time to come up with whatever it is you need to come up with to do what you gotta do. If you don't, I expect you and your things to be gone from this guesthouse by 9:01," Crack said, walking out the door and slamming it shut behind him.

I knew my friend was tired of my shit and if I didn't do what he and Queen wanted, I was going to be checking into a shelter Monday evening and that was something I definitely wasn't doing.

I took another long swig from the bottle and grimaced from the bitter taste of the warm liquid that always seemed to bring me so much comfort. But this time, the alcohol didn't have the effect it normally did for me. Instead, it made me realize that everything my oldest friend had said about me was nothing but the truth.

I spent the rest of my day figuring out how I was going to pull this seminar off on Monday even though I really didn't want to have anything to do with any of it, but I really had no choice unless I wanted to be looking for somewhere else to lay my head..

Maybe Crack was right. Maybe it was time for me to move on.

Chapter Twelve

I-85
Pinky York

I pulled into a Quick Trip gas station and filled up my tank on my bike. According to my GPS, I was only a few miles outside of Atlanta. I still hadn't figured out what I was doing here. I had driven nine hours to Georgia from D.C. on a whim. I took my pink helmet off and fished around in my back pocket for the admission form I had copied with Neko's address on it and read the address again.

I had never been the type to pine away for a man, but there was something special about Neko. *He's worth this,* I thought as I folded the paper and stuffed it back into the pocket of my jeans.

I went inside the gas station and paid for my gas and bought a small coffee. I had driven all the way here without resting and the nine hour ride was starting to take its toll on me. As I walked out to pump my gas, I passed by a middle-aged Latina woman who was on her phone while she headed back to her own vehicle.

I don't know why I noticed her or why I even paid her any mind at all. My eyes followed her as she switched in her designer shades and expensive attire. I watched as she got into her late model Benz; that's when I noticed she wasn't alone. There was a young woman on the passenger side of the car who instantly grabbed my attention.

The young woman was staring at me and I don't know why she seemed so eerily familiar to me. Her grey eyes peered at me, making me feel like I didn't belong there. The way she watched me made me feel naked. I had never been one to be intimidated by anyone, but the way the young woman looked at me made a cold chill run up my spine. A voice from the corner of my mind told me to turn around and go home. The young woman continued to watch me even as the Latina woman in the driver's seat cranked up the engine and pulled away. The girl's stare followed me long after they had left the gas station and turned on to the interstate. From where I was standing watching the tail lights of the Benz, I could see them get on the ramp marked north.

A loud click from the hose that was inserted into my tank signaled that the tank of my bike was full and it snapped me back to reality. I topped off my tank, hopped on my bike and headed into the city of Atlanta to look for a hotel. I needed to rest and gather my thoughts before I faced Neko. I had no idea what I was going to say to him once we were face to face. It had been seventeen long years. I hadn't even thought about if he were to turn me away. Then this whole trip would have been for nothing.

I drove through Atlanta in amazement. I had always had thoughts that the A was nothing but country folks with laid back attitudes and southern charm. I was wrong. It reminded me of D.C. with its long winding highways and huge buildings that seemed like they kissed the sky. The traffic was just as bad as Drama City's and the people were just as rude too. There was nothing country about the residents except their southern drawl.

When I made it to the Holiday Inn at the airport I was amped up. I should have been ready to rest, but I was wide awake. I blamed it on the coffee I had before I got into the city. I checked into my room and showered and went to the information desk in the lobby to inquire about some hot spots around town. The clerk told me about a new spot in Stockbridge about twenty minutes from the hotel that was supposed to be poppin'. She said all the reality television stars hung out there.

The clerk gave me directions to the G Street Bar and Lounge and went about her business checking other guests in. I took the piece of paper she had written the directions on and put them in my GPS and made my way through the city until I pulled up in front of the bar. I killed the engine on my bike and strolled in the doors of the bar. The first thing I noticed upon entering was the big screen televisions and the pool tables that covered the majority of the establishment. The entire bar was packed from wall to wall with people. After shuffling through few hundred people, I made my way to the bar and tried to get one of the three bartender's attention. They were running back and forth pouring drinks, taking orders and scooping up tips left behind from other patrons. When I was about to give up on my mission to get a drink, a gentleman in his late thirties or early forties called out to one of the bartenders. The scantily-dressed woman behind the bar quickly made her way down to where the man was standing next to me.

"What can I get for you, Mr. Hudson?" the woman said, batting her long, false lashes.

"I think our guest wants to order a drink," the man said to the woman who just a few minutes before had completely ignored me.

The woman took my order and offered her apologies and went about her business of fulfilling my order.

"I apologize for the service this evening. We have several celebrity authors in the building this evening so it's kind of crazy in here," the man explained in his southern drawl.

"Damn...authors pull in this type of crowd? Maybe I've been in the wrong business all my life," I said dryly.

"What kind of business are you in?" the stranger asked me, making casual conversation and holding me captive with his friendly demeanor.

I started to speak then I stopped and thought long and hard about what I was about to say. "Maybe I should write a book about what I do...I mean, what I did..." I said chuckling.

"Maybe you should. If you've got a story to tell, then maybe you should tell it. The question is: is it a good story?" Mr. Hudson asked, smiling an infectious smile that caused me to smile back at him.

"I don't know if anyone would even be interested in reading it *if* I were to write it."

"As long as the story is good, trust me, people will read it," the man said.

"How do you know? Are you and expert in that field? Besides, I wouldn't know how my story would even end," I said to him flatly.

He didn't say anything. He pulled out a business card which read *George Sherman Hudson, CEO of G Street Entertainment*. "As long as you've got a good story, people will read it. Once you work on that ending, give me a call. We'll see about getting that book turned into something special," he said.

Just before I started to ask him another question, the bartender made her way back with my drink and placed it and the tab in front of me. Mr. Hudson slid the tab back over to the bartender and told her that my tab was on the house. The bartender rolled her eyes and sauntered away. She probably knew there would be no tip for her included in that tab.

"I got your drinks tonight since you had troubles

getting your drink in the first place. Make sure you work on that ending and once you have it just right, give us a call. Everyone has at least one good story to tell," Mr. Hudson winked and walked away.

I turned the card over and read that the man who so graciously paid for my drink was into music, books, publishing, movies and other seemingly lucrative ventures. When I looked up to ask the mystery man a question, he had dipped off into the crowd of people. I tucked his card into my bra and thought about what I had said to him. My life would make good book or movie; but as I had said before, I didn't know how it was going to play out. Hopefully, I would get my happy ending before I left Atlanta and then I would have a great story to tell.

After several drinks and purchasing a few books from the authors who were inside the bar hustling, I left. I had to get back to my hotel and rest so I could be ready to make my way to Neko and hopefully my destiny.

*****

The next morning I got up early and got dressed. Today was the day that I had done all of this driving for; I was going to see Neko. I had no real plan of action and that scared me. When I pulled up in front of his three-story home that sat on the outskirts of Atlanta, I was a bit hesitant. I even thought about turning around and going back to D.C. I must've been crazy for coming all this way on impulse. I got off of my bike walked up the walkway and stood in front of the door trying to make up my mind. I didn't know if I should stay or go. I was about to hop on my bike and leave when the front door of the house opened and Neko walked out on the porch. When our eyes connected it was if he had seen a ghost. The cup of coffee he was holding in his hands slipped from his hands and smashed against the concrete into a million pieces. The warm liquid spattered all over my legs and clothes. We stood there eyeing each other for what felt like an eternity, but neither one of us said a word.

I inspected his face and it was definitely Neko. He hadn't changed much. His grey eyes were still intense and inviting. The only difference was that he had aged a little and now he sported a beard that had a few flecks of grey hair that shone through; giving him a distinguished look.

"It can't be," he muttered. He was clearly shocked to see me. After all, I was dead as far as he knew.

I tossed my signature long pink locks to the side and swallowed the lump that had formed in my throat. "I didn't mean to pop up on you unexpectedly, Neko, but I had to find you. I needed to see you. I had to get my ending," I stammered. I knew I sounded like a lunatic, but I didn't know what else to say.

"Pinky? But you're dead! I mean...they said you were dead. What kind of game is this?" he asked confused, but never taking his eyes off of me. I felt uneasy from the way he scanned me from head to toe as if to make sure I wasn't an imposter.

"It's no game, Neko. I'm very much alive. I came here from D.C. to see you. I needed to get some closure and my...ending..." my voice trailed off. I never rehearsed what I was going to say to him. I knew I sounded foolish and wasn't making a bit of sense to him.

"But the police said you died seventeen years ago, Pinky. How did you end up on my porch in Georgia?" he asked confused.

I shook my head back and forth. I hated hearing him say he thought I was dead. My head started to throb. I felt one of those damn headaches coming on. I rubbed my temples and looked at Neko with pleading eyes. I needed him to hear me out.

"No, Neko. The police told you I was dead to protect me. They said they were protecting me from whoever *tried* to kill me back then. If you give me a few minutes, I can explain," I said, hoping he would give me the time I so desperately needed to explain what happened.

"Yeah, Pinky I think you should explain. Explain why you are just showing up after all this time. Explain how you even found me. Why now? After all this time...why now?"

I swallowed the bile that was trying to make its way up and out. I didn't have the answers he wanted and deserved. I had come here on a whim. Before I could find the right words to say, Neko grabbed me by my elbow and pulled me into the house. Once I was inside, I watched as he stuck his head out the front door to make sure no one saw him pull me inside. The first thing I noticed once we were inside was the pictures that lined the foyer. I thought for sure I was going to blow chunks on the floor. The first picture I saw was a picture of Neko and the same Latina woman I had seen the night before at the Quick Trip. It was his wife. What were the odds that I had run into her the night before? The next picture that I saw was a framed graduation photo of the same young woman who had accompanied his wife the night before. I don't know how I hadn't seen it before. The young woman was his niece YaSheema Nicole. I knew she looked familiar when I saw her last night, but I hadn't been able to put two and two together. I was so concerned with the woman driving the Benz that I didn't take the time to see that his niece was staring me in the face.

"Pinky...Pinky..."

I snapped out of my thoughts and focused in on Neko who was calling my name. He was trying to get me to follow him. We entered into a sitting room that was big enough for me to fit my entire apartment in. I took a seat on the beautiful white couch and tried to fight the urge to get up and run out of there. I knew I didn't belong there. The pictures that lined his hallway told me so. I had no place in his life. He had moved on without me and I was sitting there looking crazy, chasing hopes and dreams of being with a man that had gone on with his life. I mean...what was he supposed to do...pine away for me forever? I was dead as far as he knew. I guess I wanted him to be in love with me forever.

Neko took a seat next to me and his eyes peered at me with so much confusion and curiosity it made me cower away from him just a bit when he reached for my hand. “Pinky, I have so many questions. Where have you been the last seventeen years that you’re just now reaching out to me?” Neko asked tenderly.

The way he stroked my hand put me at ease. I calmed down just a bit and swallowed the lump that formed in my throat and prevented me from speaking. “Neko, the last night I spoke with you, I was in a horrible accident. I was on my way to see you when the brakes on my bike gave out and I was struck by a truck. When I woke up in the hospital days later, my life was different. The police were all around and they said you tried to find me but they told you that I was dead. They said they had done it to protect me,” I said getting misty eyed reliving how my life was stolen from me.

“I don’t understand why would they tell me you were dead?”

I cleared my throat and wiped the tears that were threatening to break free like a sweet Georgia rain. “Someone tried to kill me that night. I don’t know who, but someone cut my brake line on my bike and at that moment, the assassin became the target. Someone tried to take me out. They didn't count on me surviving that accident; and if I had known my life would have been like this, I would rather have died," I said truthfully.

There was no controlling the tears now. I let them fall freely, unashamed of how I looked at that moment. I was always myself with Neko and now was no different. He knew who I really was deep down inside and I never had to front or pretend with him. He had always allowed me to be a woman. He never judged me for anything I had ever done; not my career choices or anything else.

Neko reached up and wiped the tears from my face so gently I instantly remembered why I loved him. He was so completely different from any man I had ever met. Even with his father's blood coursing through his veins, he was totally opposite of his entire family. They were ruthless thugs, but Neko had a sweet and gentle air about him that soothed me. Don't get me wrong...he was definitely cut from the same cloth as his murderous sister YaYa, and he was a lover like his father the late Darnell Clayton, but he was a bit softer and maybe that was why I found myself attracted to him. Neko had that dirty Clayton DNA; however, he didn't let his family ties lead him astray.

Neko pulled me into an embrace and I could feel that the connection we shared many years ago were still there.

"Pinky, I'm glad you're alive and safe," Neko said softly as he rocked me in his strong arms and I felt all seventeen years of pain, remorse and regret melt away. I needed to hear him say that he was happy to be reunited with me. It meant the world to me. I held on to him, afraid that if I were to let him go he would somehow disappear.

"Neko, I need you. I need to know that we can make things right between us. Please tell me we still have a chance at a future together," I blurted out. Neko let go of me and stared at me like there were a million things he wanted to say. He pulled away from me and shook his head.

"Pinky, I'm married now. I have a life in Georgia. I can't hurt Rhina. She has been riding for me since the day I lost you and I can't disappoint her," Neko mumbled. Then he went on to tell me about his niece and his crazy sister NiQue and how Dread had left their daughter on him to raise.

I heard every word he said, but that wasn't going to stop me from getting what I had come here for. I wanted my man and I was determined to have him at any cost. I saw my chance and looked him in his warm eyes and brought his face closer to mine and pressed my lips against his. It felt so good to taste him again. The familiarity of Neko soothed me; and to my surprise, he didn't pull away. Instead, he kissed me back. Our tongues danced a forbidden dance and I knew I had him right back where we left off. His kiss told me he still loved me as much as I loved him. His hands roved over my body and I trembled with delight as his wicked tongue found the spot on my neck that he remembered drove me wild.

We were so caught up in each other that even the loud knocking on the door couldn't stop us. Only when the knocking turned to loud, hard banging is when he pulled away from the devious things we were about to do. Neko hopped up off the couch with the speed of lighting and rushed to the front door. When he returned to the sitting room, I was sure he was ready to continue what we'd started, but I couldn't have been more wrong. Neko wasn't alone. Two uniformed police officers were right on his heels and I could tell from the scowl on their faces, they weren't there on a social call.

Chapter Thirteen

Final Destination
YaSheema Nicole

I don't know who the female was that stared me down at the Quick Trip, but something told me she was someone I knew or was going to know in the future. I really didn't want to take this long trip to D.C. with Rhina, but what other choice did I have? Uncle Neko was on some ill shit and I had to get to school to start my life and find my father.

"What are you over there thinking about?" Rhina asked, breaking into my private thoughts.

"Nothing. How much longer before we get there? I'm sick of being in the car," I replied dryly. Rhina and I had been in the car for at least seven hours and I was getting anxious.

"We only have a few more hours before we make it to the Chocolate City. I'm really excited for you, YaSheema. Howard is a great school. D.C.is unlike anything you have ever seen in Georgia. I'm sure you're gonna love it."

"Good. Can we stop for a little while? I need to stretch my legs and if I have to eat one more cold sandwich, I'm gonna hurl," I said making faces.

Rhina nodded her head and starting getting over so she could get off at the next exit. We passed a sign that read: *Welcome to Richmond* and I hoped that it meant we weren't too far from our final destination. We got off the exit and pulled up at a Sheraton.

"Do you think we can stay here overnight? Maybe we can check out the city and see what Richmond has to offer," I suggested, hoping Rhina would be down for the cause.

"Sure. I don't mind. Let me go check us in and we can find out what we can get in to," Rhina smiled brightly as she exited the car.

"I hope she doesn't think this lil' road trip is gonna make me like her," Takiya said.

I tensed up hearing her voice. She had been quiet since earlier and I wasn't excited to hear from her now.

"Look, Takiya...you've been quiet this long, I hope you will keep quiet until we shake her okay?" I said, attempting to keep Takiya at bay.

"Why don't we shake the ole bitch now? While she's in the hotel checking in, we can just pull off. By the time anyone finds out we've gone, we'll be in D.C." Takiya said with excitement in her voice.

"You know we can't do no shit like that. If we leave her, Uncle Neko will be on the first thing smoking to find us."

Trying to reason with Takiya was becoming a daily chore and since I wasn't being paid for it, I wasn't interested in doing it.

"What can Uncle Neko do to us and he's in Atlanta? Knowing him, he's back at home knee-deep in some stripper's pussy," Takiya laughed wickedly.

"Watch your mouth! That's my uncle you're talking about. I don't care how you feel about him; he's still my blood! That man raised me and even if you don't like it or understand that he's the only person that loved me enough to take me in...you will respect it!" I said, getting Takiya straight. She wasn't going to ruin this for me. She was already skating on thin ice with me especially if what she said earlier was true; then she had left a nigga' leaking back in Georgia and I still hadn't completely digested that. She should just sit back and be quiet before she really pissed me off.

Takiya settled down when Rhina returned to the car smiling widely with a keycard in her hand. "Come on. We're all checked in. I think stopping here was a good idea. I got an adjoining suite so you can have your privacy," Rhina said pulling one of her suitcases from the trunk.

I got out and grabbed my roll bag with my toiletries in it. I followed Rhina to our room and she went into her side of the suite and I went into mine. I closed the door and put my bag on the bed so I could find something to change into after I took a shower. Knowing Aunt Rhina, she wasn't going to want to go anywhere I would have wanted to go. She was so stuck up that she would have us in some snobbiest restaurant in Richmond instead of a happening bar. That's just how Rhina was.

I pulled out a pair of black jeans, a simple button up shirt and got in the shower. When I got out, I heard Aunt Rhina's shower on her side of the suite come alive. She started singing in Spanish. I pushed my things to the other side of the bed and lay down. I wasn't supposed to take a nap, but that seven hour ride had worn me out.

*****

"Get up bitch! Let's go! We gotta go now!"

I sat straight up and looked around. I panicked when I didn't realize where I was. The room I was in was dark and the curtains were partially closed. My eyes darted around the room and I calmed down only when I remembered we were in a hotel. I figured I had been asleep for a few hours because the sun was up when Aunt Rhina and I had arrived at the hotel and now I didn't see any sings of the sun. From what I could see, the sun had gone down and it was dusk.

I wiped my eyes and wondered why Aunt Rhina would let me sleep so long.

"Didn't you hear me? I said we gotta go!" Takiya was practically yelling.

"I thought I told you go away," I said, brushing Takiya off. I got up and stumbled around until I found the lamp and turned it on flooding the room with artificial light.

"For someone who's supposed to be so smart, you sure are dumb. You never listen to me when I try to help your stupid ass out," Takiya fussed.

"Where's Aunt Rhina and why didn't you wake me up. You knew we were supposed to go get something to eat," I said annoyed. Takiya kept nagging me to get my things so we could go, but I continued to brushed her off. She really was starting to work on my last good nerve.

I put on my robe and walked out of my room and across the tiny living room that separated my room from Aunt Rhina's. Right as I was about to knock on Rhina's door, Takiya starting going wild.

"I told you let's go! She ain't in there!"

"Oh God, I wish you would stop with the bullshit, Takiya and just go away," I said low enough that Aunt Rhina couldn't hear me talking to myself. I lightly knocked on Rhina's door and there was no answer.

"I told you she ain't there."

I knocked again, ignoring Takiya. She truly was buggin' and I didn't know how I had put up with her so many years without going completely going crazy. There was no answer at Rhina's door and my heartbeat sped up. Something about the whole situation seemed very wrong. Even though my head told me not to open the door, my hands had a mind of their own. Slowly turning the knob, I pushed the door open and was immediately met by a very familiar odor. It was one I had smelled twenty-four hours before. It was a metallic and pungent and it made my stomach do flip-flops.

On sight, everything seemed like it was fine until I stepped further into the room. My legs felt like jelly as I rounded the bed. On the other side of the bed was Aunt Rhina. Her body laid face-up and her eyes were wide open. As I scanned the rest of her, my inspection didn't get far before I saw the blood that poured from each of the puncture wounds that were all over her lower torso.

"What the fuck?!" I screamed in shock as I ran to Rhina's side and cradled her in my arms, rocking her like a newborn baby.

"I told you, you didn't want to come in here; didn't I?" Takiya said nonchalantly.

"What the fuck did you do? Why would you do something like this?" I asked over and over as I held Rhina hoping that she was only unconscious. From the blank stare on her face I could tell that she was beyond unconscious. She was gone and where she had drifted to there was no returning.

"You might want to come on before them boys in blue figure out what happened here and bust *our* ass. Let's go...NOW!" Takiya demanded.

I didn't move. Instead, I continued rocking Aunt Rhina. "I'm sorry, Rhina. I'm so, so, so sorry. I didn't mean for any of this to happen. Please wake up."

"I'm sure you know, just like I know, that she can't hear you. The bitch is dead and out of our way. Now I would suggest you get off of your ass and clean yourself up, and let's get out of here before the maid comes sniffing around talking about clean towels and shit. Now let's go!"

I sat there for what seemed like an eternity before I felt like I was all cried out. At some point during my meltdown, Takiya had finally quieted down and shut up all together. I can't say that her finally going on about her business was better, because now I felt all alone. I sat there with Aunt Rhina's dead, lifeless body in my lap until I heard a soft knock on the door. Pushing Rhina gently to the side, I got to my feet and ran to the door into our suite and prayed no one came in.

"Housekeeping," I heard the voice say through the door right as I got to it. I heard what sounded like someone fumbling with the door and I pressed my body against the door in an attempt to keep the maid out. If she gained access to this room, she was gonna find more than a few dirty towels and sheets.

"Umm, we don't need anything ma'am. We're just fine," I said in an attempt to get the woman to go away.

"Well, next time chu' need to put up the *Do not disturb* sign, ok," the aggravated woman shot back. Her voice was in a thick Latin accent that instantly made me think of my dead Aunt Rhina whose body was growing cold in the next room.

"I told you *we* should have gotten out of here! But no, you wanna sit around here holding that bitch like ya'll were the best of friends, when in fact you hated that spic bitch as much as I did!"

"Shut the fuck up, Takiya! Just shut the fuck up and let me think. I need to figure out how *we're* gonna get out of here," I said rubbing my temples. The truth was I really didn't know what to do next. I thought about calling Uncle Neko and telling him what happened, but quickly decided against that because he would surely turn me in to the police. This wasn't some random chick that was lying dead in the next room, it was his wife. He would never forgive me for this.

"I know what *we're* gonna do. You're gonna take your ass in the bathroom and take another shower. You're gonna wash Rhina off of your body and then *we* are gonna get the fuck out of here. *We're* gonna drive to Washington, D.C. and you're gonna check in for school like none of this shit ever happened. When her body is found, you can say ya'll got into an argument and you kept going to D.C. without her.

I shook my head from left to right. "That will never work. What about DNA, Takiya? They're gonna fry my ass because of you. I'm sure this hotel has cameras. Someone saw me come in here with her. Now what about that, huh? You got all of the answers. What are your answers for that?" I asked, making more noise than I had intended to make.

"YaSheema, I have all of that figured out. You and

Rhina had a fight in the hotel and you left. Simple as that. Your DNA should be on her dummy. That's your aunt or did you forget? Now go do what I told you to do and I will handle the rest. I got you. I promise they ain't gonna pin this shit on you. You forget that if they pin it on you, I'm going down with you too and you know damn well I ain't gonna let that happen," Takiya assured me.

Feeling defeated, I did as I was told even though I didn't think it was the best thing to do. I showered and put all of my things back in my bag. I slid on the clothes I was wearing when I first entered the hotel and took my things to the door as Takiya instructed me to do.

"Now what?" I asked her, standing there with my hand on the knob waiting on further instructions.

"Go get her wallet and take whatever cash she has, her credit cards and the car keys and we can be out of here. Simple as that."

Takiya made it sound like *we* hadn't committed a murder. She made it sound like it wasn't as complex as it really was. I had seen Shonda Rhimes hit show, *How to Get Away With Murder* but I didn't think I could live it. I wasn't built like this.

Instead of protesting, I went back into Rhina's tomb and snatched her wallet off of the dresser along with the car keys and dashed out of the room. The smell of death followed me and I wanted to shake it. When I got back to the main door, I didn't bother to wait for Takiya to instruct me. Instead, I grabbed my shit and darted out the door putting the *Do not disturb* tag on the knob and dashed down the hallway. I half expected to see the Virginia State Police waiting for me, but they weren't.

"Calm down. If you do something stupid all you're gonna do is draw attention to *us*. Slow down and act as if everything is normal."

I did as Takiya instructed this time and slowed down my pace. As calmly as I could, I walked out of the hotel, hoping no one knew my dirty little secret. Keeping my head lowered, I walked across the parking lot and opened the door to the car. Once I threw my bag inside, I got in and pulled off.

"Good job, YaSheema. I knew *we* could do it. I mean...I knew you could do it. Maybe you're tougher than I ever gave you credit for," Takiya sang in my ear.

Her voice made me cringe and all I wanted was a little peace and quiet. I turned the stereo on and headed back the way Rhina and I had come off of the interstate. I don't think I breathed until I was on I-95 north. If I could make it to D.C., then maybe I could try to start over and put this whole mess behind me.

Chapter Fourteen

History Repeats Itself
Neko Reynolds

Today was one surprise after another. First, the woman I thought was dead showed up on my front porch and now the police was here asking me questions about YaSheema Nicole.

"Mr. Reynolds, we don't mean to disturb you, but we have a few questions about your niece. It shouldn't take any more than a few moments of your time," the fat, balding detective said eyeing Pinky. His partner was a tall black woman who looked as though she had ten million better things to do than to be here questioning us about YaSheema. I could tell by her body language that she was going to be the bad cop. She had angry black woman's syndrome written all over her. I nodded my head in their direction and hoped they made whatever this was about quick. I had my ex-lover sitting in my living room and she had absolutely no business being here. If Rhina were to walk in right now, I would surely have some explaining to do and I know she wouldn't want to hear shit about Pinky being just a friend. Rhina may have loved me endlessly, but she wasn't going to stand for me trying to play her.

I looked over at Pinky and she shifted uncomfortably on the couch, but I assumed her curiosity about the cops being in my house made her sit right there like she was watching a real live freak show.

"Mr. Reynolds, where was your niece last night?" the male detective asked.

"She was out with her friends. They went out since it was her last night in town before she left for school. I think they hit a few parties and then she came home. Why?" I asked curiously.

"We have reason to believe she was involved in an altercation with a security guard at one of the clubs she visited," the female detective said, never giving her partner the opportunity to finish his question.

"What kind of altercation? I ain't never known detectives to go through all of this over an argument," I said growing worrisome. From the tone of the female detective's voice, there was much more to their visit than an altercation.

"Well, Mr. Reynolds...the bouncer from the club is dead and several people from the club – including her friend Cassandra and her friend Vernita – said your niece said some very vicious things to the bouncer that would cause some concern. Now may we speak to her so we can clear this all up?" the female detective said gruffly.

I was no rocket scientist, but I knew they weren't there just to question YaSheema about an argument. They were there to interrogate her and accuse her of the bouncer's death. The male detective seemed to have a much calmer demeanor than his partner and I knew he was the one I should reason with.

"Look...she isn't here. My wife and my niece left to drive YaSheema to school in Washington, D.C. I can assure you that my niece didn't have anything to do with that man's death; and unless you have some concrete proof...I suggest you both leave my house," I said growing irritated with the female detective's nasty attitude. She knew nothing about my niece and she was basically accusing her of a crime that I was sure YaSheema didn't commit. She was being the judge and the jury and she didn't even have any evidence besides some he say she say crap. The female detective looked over in Pinky's direction and smirked. I guess after she heard me mention my wife, she thought she had me all figured out.

I walked out into the foyer toward the front door to let the detectives out. I didn't think it would be in my best interest to say anything else to them. I didn't know what happened, and it would be stupid to say anything more to them without speaking to YaSheema and our attorney first. I had been through more than enough legal troubles in my past to know not to say too much.

I opened the front door wide and the two detectives

took that as their queue to get the fuck out of my house. The male detective shook his head as if he were embarrassed that he had even come into my home for this madness. He handed me his card and apologized for taking up my time. I nodded and waited for his overgrown man-ish female counterpart to join him.

When she made it to the door, she smirked at me again. "Make sure that you have your niece and your *wife* contact us as soon as possible," she said, glancing back into the sitting room where Pinky was sitting listening to every word she said. Then the detective handed me her card which I refused to take and she dropped it at my feet and walked out. I was so pissed off with her smug behavior that I slammed the front door so hard that all the pictures on the wall clanged on their hinges when the door slammed shut.

I took a deep breath and re-entered the sitting room where Pinky was still seated. She was staring at me with so much concern on her face that I couldn't look at her. I was ashamed for what almost happened right before the police had broken up our good time. I had worked hard to change my life and be a good husband to my wife and now my dead ex was sitting in my living room.

"Neko, what are you gonna do about that? That bitch cop was practically accusing your niece of murder," Pinky said finally speaking up.

"I'm gonna call my wife and make her bring YaSheema Nicole back home so we can clear this bullshit up. As for you...you cannot be here when my wife returns with my niece," I said with more attitude than I intended to have. I snatched my phone off of the mantle and punched Rhina's cell phone number in. The phone just rang. I hung up and called her again with no answer. After calling her four more times without getting any answer, I knew something was seriously wrong. Rhina practically kept that phone attached to her ear. Even when she was driving she had it hooked up through the stereo system speakers so she could use the phone hands free while driving.

I slammed the phone on the table out of frustration and fear for my family. Something was wrong and every bad feeling I had suppressed for the last seventeen years was making its way to the surface and threatening to break free.

"Neko, I didn't come here to get in your way. I only came here to tell you that I'm alive. I wasn't trying to ruin whatever it is you think you got with your wife. I only came here for my closure. I needed it. I have lived seventeen years dead on the inside and the only thing that kept me alive was the hope of finding you to tell you I love you," Pinky said. She lowered her eyes and I know it took a lot for her to drive from D.C. to tell me that.

Pinky had never been the warm and fuzzy type and it was apparent that the last seventeen years had been hard on her and she had changed. She was no longer the person I knew years ago. I knew I felt something for her. I had never really stopped loving her, but that was in the past. I was married with my own family and it was time for her to let go of whatever feeling she harbored for me. I was determined to never let my father's DNA that coursed through my veins to cause me any more pain. My father, Darnell, was a man-whore and I had almost slipped into his ways when I was younger. Hell, I almost slipped into them right before the cops showed up at my front door.

"Pinky, it's good to see you, but I'm sure you know I got other things going on and I really don't have time for this now. I need to find my wife and niece so we can clear up this misunderstanding," I said, walking to the front door. I was hoping that she would get the hint and make her exit easy on both of us. I didn't need any complications. When I got to the front door, Pinky wasn't behind me. Instead, she was standing up in the sitting area with a grim look on her face.

"So, that's it? You were two seconds from sexing me up before the cops came in and now you wanna be a family man? I ain't never understood you, Neko. I honestly don't know why I bothered giving a fuck then and I don't know why I give a fuck now. I guess I was hoping that you lived these last seventeen years missing me the way I missed you," she said with tears threatening to break free from her eyes.

This was definitely a different Pinky. She had never been the type to wear her emotions on her sleeve. Maybe I had dismissed her a little too harshly. I closed the front door and walked back into the sitting room and tried to make Pinky understand that I was a different man from the one that I was when she disappeared. What we had started before could never be finished. I could never betray Rhina. I walked over to Pinky and put my arms around her and held her tightly.

"Pink, I will always have love for you, girl. You were the first woman I ever loved. Things are different now. I am married and I built something special with Rhina and I could never leave her."

"I know, Neko. I know. I just thought that if I came here, you would miss me as much as I missed you and we could start over," she said, pushing her signature pink locs out of her face. The more I inspected Pinky, the more I realized I really loved this woman. She was different, but she was still familiar to me and I wanted her, but I didn't want to hurt my wife. I was torn between doing what was right and doing what I knew my heart wanted me to do.

Pinky broke free from my embrace and wiped her tears away. "I guess it's a good thing I came here when I did. You might need me. If your niece is in trouble, then maybe I could help. Neko, I think I saw your wife and niece when I was on my way into Atlanta. Your wife was at a Quick Trip gas station and your niece was with her. I didn't know who they were until I saw the pictures on the wall in the hallway, but there was something eerily familiar about your niece when I saw her. I don't know why I knew she was familiar to me then since I hadn't seen her since..." her voice trailed off.

"That means they're alright then," I interjected. I scratched my head and another thought popped in my head.

"How did you find me, Pinky? After all these years, how did you know to come here and find me again?" I quizzed.

"I work for Howard University. I work in the admission's department. I am in charge of your niece's housing and when her paperwork came across my desk with your name on it, I dropped everything, left work and came straight here to find you."

"Well, I might need your help. We need to pay her friends a visit so I can find out what happened that night she went to the club. I need to know why they would tell the cops they thought YaSheema would have something to do with that security guard's death. Maybe Rhina will call me back by then. Either way, we need to find out as much as we can and then find my wife and YaSheema Nicole before the police catch up to them," I suggested.

Pinky nodded her head and picked her bag up off the floor and dug around in it until she found her pink glock and checked to make sure it was ready for action in case she needed it. I couldn't help but smile. Some things never changed and for some strange reason, I was happy that they hadn't. Pinky may have aged a little bit, but she was still ready to make it do what it do if she had to; and for that I was grateful. She had always been a rider and lethal if she needed to be and somehow that comforted me in the craziest way. I guess the more things changed, the more they stayed the same; especially if you were a part of my life. I just hoped my past wasn't repeating itself.

Chapter Fifteen

Uneasy
Dread

I hated everything about Mondays; especially now that I had to get up and work like a real person. This wasn't for me and I knew it. If I looked back to when I was younger, I would have never thought I would be doing a real 9-5 job for the sake of saving my life.

Queen had already called me twice and told me that I had better have my ass up and ready to head to Howard to be briefed on what I was supposed to be doing my lectures on. The actual classes didn't start until a week from today, but I had to meet the other department heads and staff. I honestly didn't want to meet anyone and I damn sure didn't want to leave the comfort of my bed and bottle. *Fuck this work shit!*

I got up and showered, hoping that I could wash the weed and liquor stench that was coming from my pores. I brushed my teeth, gargled, squeezed the last of my Visine in my eyes and headed out the door after wrestling with my tie for twenty minutes. I knew if I didn't leave soon, Queen was going to have a lot to say about it and I didn't feel like hearing her shit this morning, or any other morning for that matter.

I braved the D.C. traffic which was horrible. All the stop and go from Benning Road to Florida Avenue was enough to drive a sane nigga insane. The unnecessary trolley cars, which were a waste of the tax payer's money, and the rude drivers were all annoying me. Considering I was on the brink of insanity already, the entire trip was a headache. When I pulled into the faculty parking lot of the university, I was ready to twist up a J and smoke just to calm me down; but then I remembered I left my weed at home so I wouldn't be tempted.

I cursed at myself for not bringing my smoke with me and walked to the administrative offices where I was supposed to meet Ms. Grey. By the time I found her office, I was already twenty minutes late and I really didn't give a fuck. She should have been glad that I showed up at all. If she gave me any attitude about my tardiness, I would gladly tell her to kiss my ass and walk right back out the door. To my surprise, Ms. Grey didn't give me any attitude at all. She greeted me with a warm, sexy smile.

"Good morning, Mr. Evans. I'm so glad you accepted my offer. I was super excited when Queen told me you would be joining us. We can head up to the conference room where you will be introduced to the other staff. I'm sure you'll love them. I've been here for the past eight years and I have enjoyed my time with them. You'll also meet the admission's director and your assistant who will be able to help you with anything you'll need to get you started. Of course classes don't start until next week, but we should be able to get you up to speed on things before then," Ms. Grey said, handing me a binder.

She stood up and I immediately took notice of the midnight blue dress she was wearing that hugged her thick hips in all the right places. Ms. Grey was definitely a lot to look at. She may even be worth the trip every morning as long as she kept wearing shit like that to work. Maybe this work shit wouldn't be so bad after all.

I stared at her a little too long and she caught me looking at her lustfully and she blushed. "Damn. I mean...excuse me for being late this morning, Mrs. Grey. The traffic was horrible on the way in," I said, trying to make the obviously awkward moment easier.

"Miss Grey," she said, correcting me, "Mr. Evans, and it's really no problem at all. I just got in too. You ain't gotta tell me about the traffic. I already know how it is getting to Georgia Avenue on a Monday morning. No one around here is on time," she giggled and led the way out of her office and out into the hallway.

There were students coming and going trying to get their classes and tuition situated. Ms. Grey switched in front of me and greeted several people on our way to the conference room. We spent several hours being briefed on what was expected of us during the first few weeks of classes and they went through policies and school practices before we took a break for lunch. I was surprised that I managed to stay awake during the whole four-hour ordeal. I ain't gonna' lie, I did more watching of Ms. Grey than anything else. She was throwing glances my way and flashing me her killer smile; and I know that was the only thing keeping me even remotely alert.

When we were all filing out for our break, Ms. Grey was outside of the conference room waiting for me. "See, I told you it wasn't gonna be so bad. Now for the best part of the day...lunch! Since it's your first day, I thought I would treat you to lunch. Do you like Italian? There's a little bistro around the corner that has the best pasta and they serve the best wine around," she suggested, nudging me. At the sound of anything alcoholic, I was interested. She didn't have to ask me twice. I nodded my head and let her lead the way.

Ms. Grey and I headed back to the administrative offices and passed by the admission's office. Ms. Grey wanted to grab her purse and car keys. I waited in front of the admission's desk where there was a line of students waiting to speak to someone about their housing assignments. That's when I noticed her. I felt like all of the wind had been knocked out of me. Surely my mind had to be playing tricks on me.

At the head of the admissions and housing line

there was a tall, shapely young woman with reddish-blondish hair and grey eyes waiting for keys to her dorm. Even after seventeen years of not being in my daughter's life, I knew it was her. She looked just like her aunt and her mother. I had to be mistaken. I just had to be. The last time I checked, my daughter YaSheema Nicole was in Georgia with her uptight ass Uncle Neko. There was no way this young woman was my daughter. It just had to be a look-a-like.

I inched a little bit closer to the line where all of the students were waiting to be helped and hoped I could see a name on the form the young woman was filling out while the other woman was surfing through a box of keys.

"Ms. Evans, these are your keys and you only get one set. If you lose them, you will be required to pay a twenty dollar replacement fee for them. I suggest you get a duplicate made for emergencies," I heard the woman at the admissions desk tell the young woman who I now knew was my daughter. I know there are thousands of people with the last name of Evans on the planet, but I am sure there aren't that many who looked just like my dead girlfriend and my dead fiancée.

I watched in amazement as the woman I believed to be my daughter took the keys from the grumpy woman behind the desk and started off in the direction of the dorms. I wanted to call after her, but my lips felt like they were glued shut. I wanted to chase behind her and introduce myself, but my feet were planted in one spot on the floor. Even if I were to catch up to her, I still wouldn't know what to do or say. What were the odds of my daughter coming back to D.C.? Would she even be willing to speak to me? After all, I had left her like she was nothing. She probably wouldn't have anything to say to me and I couldn't blame her.

I was deep in thought when Ms. Grey tapped me on my shoulder to let me know she was ready to go. "Are you ready to go, Mr. Evans?"

I must have looked totally blown because Ms. Grey stared at me with her intense, dark eyes. They were asking what was wrong, but she never actually let the words leave her lips. "Did you change your mind about lunch? If you aren't feeling it we can postpone," Ms. Grey suggested.

I hated to tell her that I had to bail on her, but I didn't think lunch was a good idea anymore. Suddenly, I wasn't hungry and all I wanted was to be alone.

"Actually, I think I will have to postpone. I need to make a phone call. It can't wait," I said, fidgeting with my tie. It felt like the walls were closing in on me and suddenly I couldn't breathe. "I've got some business to tend to. Maybe we can do lunch tomorrow. I'll catch up to you during the second part of the briefing," I said, backing away from her and out of the same doors I believed I had just seen my daughter leaving out of.

I hurried out of the school's main doors and into the parking lot. My eyes scanned the entire lot for

YaSheema Nicole, but she was nowhere to be found. I walked defeated to the employee lot and got inside my car.

"Fuck!" I yelled, punching the steering wheel. I was such a complete fuck up. I had the chance to possibly speak to my daughter again and I blew it. Cranking up the car, I decided I would have lunch after all. Maybe I would have a liquid lunch. I drove two blocks up Georgia Avenue and parked in front of the first liquor store on my side of the street. I definitely needed a drink if I was expected to make it through the rest of this day.

*****

Two hours later

When I finally looked up, I noticed two hours had gone by. I cursed under my breath and tried to get myself together. I had to finish this day and pretend I was enjoying it. Somehow I had managed to buy and consume two fifths of Remy Martin VSOP and now I was so drunk I could probably get everyone in the conference room drunk from the alcohol spewing from my pores. I never meant to drink that much. I was supposed to only have a drink or two; not have two whole bottles of brown liquor. I knew the rest of my day was going to be a challenge. I almost took my drunken ass home and deal with Queen and Crack when the time came. That's what my head was saying, but my heart was telling me that I better not fuck this up or I could end up pissing off the only two people I had left in my corner.

I dug around in my glove box and found a bottle of cheap cologne I kept there in case the feds pulled me over while I was smoking. I did my best to cover up the smell of the booze. When I was about to exit the car so I wouldn't be too late rejoining the others, my phone started to ring. When I looked at the number on the screen I rolled my eyes seeing Queen's name flash across my phone. She was calling to check in on me. I almost let the call go to voicemail, but I knew that would have been a grave mistake. I answered and tried to sound as if I was sober; which I definitely wasn't.

"Hello."

"Hey, Dread...or should I say Mr. Evans. How are things going on your first day?" Queen asked.

"Everything is going fine, I guess. I'm actually headed back in from lunch to finish our briefing and I should be out of here at about four or five o'clock," I responded, trying my very best to sound as sober as humanly possible. If Queen found out I was drunk that would be my ass.

"Good. I'm glad things are working out for you. I knew if you jumped back in the saddle you would have no problem riding this thing all the way out," she said cheerfully. She had no idea that only two minutes before she had called me I was contemplating saying fuck all of this song and dance and roll out.

"Yeah, things are going great," I lied.

"I'm glad to hear that, Dread. I knew this would be a good opportunity for you to still do something you love and make strides to better yourself."

Queen sounding like a cheerleader was blowing my high and I wanted to hang up on her. I knew how to get rid of her though.

"Queen, I am heading back in to our briefing from lunch and I don't want to be late. I'll see you and Crack when I get home and we can talk about my day then," I said, rushing her off the phone. I had absolutely no intentions of going straight home and talking about my shitty day. I said my goodbye's to Queen and sat there looking at my phone. I scrolled through the contacts and found a number I vowed I would never call. I pushed on the name *Neko Reynolds* and held my breath. It was time to find out if the young woman I saw earlier today was my daughter. I needed confirmation that she was back in D.C.

Chapter Sixteen

School Dayz
YaSheema Nicole

Somehow I had managed to make it to Washington, D.C. with no incident. I spent the rest of my drive into D.C. peering in the rearview mirror thinking that the police were following me. I'm sure someone must've found Aunt Rhina's body by now and I was sure that they were looking for me. However, no one followed me and I made it to D.C. with no problems.

The first thing I did was check into the university on Monday morning and got my room assignment. After spending my morning in the admission's office waiting to get my keys, I went about moving my things into my dorm. It took me four hours to haul all of my things in the room by myself and when I was done. I didn't want to do anything but take a nap, but my growling stomach said otherwise. After showering in the cramped bathroom I was going to share with some stranger, I got dressed and started to head out to see what I could find to eat when a young woman, who I assumed was my roomie, entered my room with a bunch of bags in her hands. She had two middle-age people who I assumed were her parents with her. The young woman dropped her things on the floor and stuck her hand out to greet me. "Hi. My name is Paige. I guess you're my roomie, YaSheema?"

I didn't shake her hand; I just looked at her and wondered how she knew my name.

Act cool dummy. They probably told her your name in the admission's office. Say hello or something. Don't just stare at her like she's a freak before she thinks something is wrong with you! Takiya broke into my thoughts and demanded.

I did as I was told and shook the young woman's hand. "Hi, yes...I'm YaSheema. I'm sorry they didn't tell me you were coming today. I guess you kind of startled me. Did you need help with your things? I just got all of my things in myself so I know what a hassle it can be," I offered, even thcugh I didn't want to help her do shit. If I had to unload and unpack my shit on my own, then she was on her own too.

"Naw, that's why my parents are here. That... and to make sure I ain't bunking with a serial killer," Paige giggled. "You know how parents are. This is my second year here and they still treat me like a damn baby," Paige whispered.

I'm glad she thought that shit was funny. I could feel the color draining from my face at the mention of serial killer and I didn't think her joke was funny at all considering I could be categorized as such.

I don't like her. You need to see what those uppity niggas in that admission's office can do about this. I don't think I'ma be able to deal with her. She's corny as fuck! Takiya said in my ear.

I did my best to ignore her and focused on my new roommate. "I'm going to head out to grab something to eat. I should be back soon," I said, by passing Paige's parents on the way out the door. Paige shook her head and her parents told me it was nice meeting me and then I left. I couldn't help but think about my own parents. I hadn't spoken with my Uncle Neko the entire weekend and I left my Aunt Rhina rotting in a hotel room.

I headed to the car and turned my cell phone on and watched as each new text message and voicemail popped up on the phone one by one. Each call and text was from Uncle Neko. I'm sure he was worried sick about me and Aunt Rhina by now. I decided not to call him back just yet because I didn't know exactly what to say to him. What was I supposed to say? Was I supposed to tell him the truth? Was I supposed to tell him that I killed his wife and continued on into D.C. like nothing ever happened? Or was I supposed to tell him that Takiya did it all? Either way, he would never believe me no matter what I told him.

"You better not tell Uncle Neko shit! He will turn our asses in and you know he will. I suggest you keep your mouth shut and let this shit play out on its own."

"And just how do you think it's gonna play out, Takiya; huh? Do you think the authorities aren't gonna figure out we were with Aunt Rhina? Do you think Uncle Neko is gonna be able to forgive *us* for what *we* did? *We* killed his wife! Then *we*... me and you got in the car and drove to D.C.; somewhere he never wanted *us* to be in the first place and checked into college like *we* didn't just kill her in cold blood. If you think that's gonna happen you're more delusional than I am, bitch!" I screamed, forgetting that it was broad daylight and people were walking by me having an open conversation with myself.

"I know you better shut the fuck up before you get *us* late before *we* even have a chance to put my plan in effect. YaSheema, just chill the fuck out and play shit real cool. Let me handle it. Now get in the car and stop acting like a fuckin' nutcase in the middle of the street before these good people hand you over to the police for actin' weird!" Takiya ordered.

I whipped my head around and noticed that a few people passing by spotted me talking to myself. I don't think they heard me, but they certainly saw me standing out in the middle of the parking lot spazzing out by my damn self.

"Shit!" I mumbled to myself. That's all I needed was for someone to see me cursing myself out and report me to campus security. Fumbling through my oversized bag, I found the car keys and hit the button to disarm the alarm.

"Damn, shawty, you aight?" I heard a voice say from behind me. I damn near jumped out of my skin. I spun around to see who had gotten in my personal space. When I came face to face with the voice I almost melted. The voice had come from a brown skin brother with a neat haircut, dressed like nothing I had seen any nigga in Georgia dressed. He was wearing nothing but a light Helly Hansen jacket and dark jeans complimented by a pair of white Air Force One's. He wasn't doing too much, but he was definitely doing enough. I locked in on his thick, brown lips and tried not to drool. He was fine. He was clean shaven and his hair was cut low. He was a breath of fresh air from what I had become accustomed to in Georgia.

"Oh umm...excuse me?" I asked the stranger, doing my best to regain my composure.

"I heard you talking to someone on your phone and I was trying to get in my car. You're blocking my door," he said, pointing at how close to the line we both were.

"Oh, my bad. I'll get out your way," I stuttered. I opened the door and slid into my car and tried not to blush from the embarrassment of how I was all up in his face.

"Naw, you're aight. Are you a freshman?" he asked me before I could shut my door.

"Yeah, I am," I knew it was too late now. I was definitely blushing and I'm sure he could see it written all over my face.

"My name is Lamont. Hey, I know you don't know me, but I was wondering if I could put my name in that phone of yours. You know...since you like to talk on it and everything, I was hoping you would talk to me too," he said smoothly.

I threw him a smile and mumbled, "Sure." I was more than happy that he assumed I was on the phone and not some deranged lunatic yelling at myself. He gave me his number and I locked it in my phone. I would definitely be calling him. He was beyond fine. "You never told me your name, beautiful."

Every time he spoke to me with his infectious smile and sexy lips, I couldn't help but blush. "My name is YaSheema Nicole, but you can call me YaSheema," I said, trying my best to hold back the goofy grin that was threatening to break free.

"Well, it sure is nice to meet you, YaSheema. I hope you'll accompany me to one of my games. I play on the varsity team and being that it's my senior year, I hope to go pro right after graduation, but we can talk about *our* future when you call me later," he said, licking his lips and causing my womanly parts to flutter. This nigga was smooth. He was a pinch too cocky, but he was doable.

"Maybe I'll see you around," I said and cranked up my car and backed out my space. I knew he was watching me. I could feel his eyes on me and I liked it.

"You better watch the road, bitch. Don't get all caught up in his ass and let's get something to eat. I don't like that pretty muthafucka' and I don't trust him. You ain't got time to be makin' googly eyes at some random nigga. We're supposed to be here on some other shit. What happened to you wanting to find your pops? I thought that was the real reason we came all the way up here." Takiya scolded me.

I heard Takiya talking, but I wasn't really listening. I was deep in my own thoughts. Maybe D.C. wasn't gonna be so bad after all.

CHAPTER SEVENTEEN

Heavy
Pinky York

I can't believe this shit. I rode all this way to pour my heart out to this nigga and he tells me he can't hurt his wife. I don't know what the fuck I was thinking about coming all this way for nothing.

What's crazier than me driving all this way to only be rejected, was the fact that I was still willing to help this nigga. I was soft on Neko and that shit never changed; even after all this time. Now, here I am, helping him track down his niece's lil' friends. He decided he had a few things he wanted to ask them before he confronted his niece...well, that's if he ever gets in touch with his niece. He's been dialing her and his wife for the last twelve hours and he hasn't gotten a response from either of them. I guess maybe Neko had run off to Georgia to settle down. Maybe he had really changed. I wish my feelings for him would change, but nope...here I am ready to ride or die for him just like old times and all he was worried about was his family.

"Neko, I know I have been out of commission for the past seventeen years, but I don't think you going to this girl Cassandra's house in the middle of the day is a good idea. Maybe we should wait for the sun to go down or something. Are you trying to let the cops know what we're doing? You know what we're doing isn't exactly legal you know?" I said, looking up and down the upper middle-class suburban street. I felt like I stuck out like a sore thumb. I don't know why I felt like all eyes were on us, but I did.

"Legal? You gotta be kidding me, Pinky! I don't think you've ever done a legal thing a day in your life. Now you wanna nitpick me about the law. I've got to find my niece and my wife. Maybe you don't understand, but my shit is different now...and it seems mighty odd that as soon as you come around, the police wanna start questioning my family about bodies and shit. How coincidental is that, Pinky?" Neko said, rubbing his temples in frustration.

"I don't know what's going on with your family Neko, but I said I would help you find them. I think you know I would never hurt your niece or your wife," I said, defending myself. He was really testing me and it was taking everything in me to stay calm.

"I don't know what I believe is true anymore. I never would have believed that I would see you again, but here you are. I don't know why I thought I could live a normal life. I ran all the way to Georgia to save my niece. But I don't think I can save her, Pink," Neko said, looking over at me from the driver seat of the car. I could see the hurt in his eyes.

"I feel like I failed YaSheema Nicole. I always thought by taking her and running away, I would save her from whatever lurked over my family. You, of all people, know my family ain't been all there. My father was no saint. My sister died for the sins of my father and my other sister was crazy as bat shit," Neko said, shaking his head. I looked over at him confused.

"What do you mean your other sister was crazy as bat shit?" I asked curiously.

Neko turned away from me and stared straight out the car window like I wasn't even there. "I don't think you want to hear this shit, Pinky. It's kind of heavy. I wouldn't believe none of this shit if I hadn't seen it with my own eyes."

"What did you see?" I asked him. My curiosity was on one hundred now. Apparently, I wasn't the only one with secrets.

"Do you remember NiQue?" he asked, never looking at me.

"Yeah. I remember her. What does she have to do with anything?"

"She was really my sister. I found out she wasn't just YaYa's friend. She was my father's dirty lil' secret. My father apparently kept my sister NiQue a secret because she was a lil' off," Neko said, shaking his head.

"A lil' off? I don't get it, Neko."

"My father kept NiQue a secret because he had no

room for a psycho in his camp. Her real name was Pajay and my father didn't think it was a good idea to be in her life, so he passed her off because she suffered from multiple personality disorder. She was fuckin' crazy to say the least; and instead of getting her the help she really needed, he paid a nigga to babysit her. Eventually she found out the truth about who she really was and then the bitch went crazy. She killed everyone I loved; then the police killed her. Then I ended up raising my niece because her father didn't want shit to do with her. I can't blame him though. That nigga had been through enough with my family. As much as I hated Dread, I can't even blame him for turning his back on his daughter. Maybe I should have turned my back on her too. I just got this fucked up feeling that history is about to repeat itself.

YaSheema Nicole has been acting weird. She hasn't been like herself, but it was familiar to me. She was acting like NiQue or ...ahh Pajay did before she died. She's been talking to herself. When I confront her about it, she acts like I'm the one who's losing it when deep down I know she is slipping into the same dark place her mother must've slipped in to. I always said that if I ever caught YaSheema Nicole acting anything like her mother, I would have her ass committed. I guess that shit was easier said than done. All the signs were right there and I should have done something. Instead, I ignored it. I hoped it wasn't the same thing my sister had gone through.

I think my sister gave into her illness because she didn't have the love she craved from our father and now I think my niece is going through the same thing. Now she's headed to D.C. to chase after her father and she's letting the illness take over her and it's all my fault. I could have stopped it, Pinky. I could have stopped it and I didn't. If anything happens to my niece, it'll be on my head. It will be my fault.

History is repeating itself. It's like this fucked up DNA that courses through my veins. It's eternal. It never ends. My father cursed us all. My family was fucked up then and I fear it just got worse with YaSheema Nicole heading to school in D.C." Neko finally looked over at me to make sure I got all that.

Oh, believe me I had questions for him; but I was still trying to chew on everything Neko said to me. I knew the Clayton-Reynolds family was fucked up. They always had been. I shouldn't have been surprised by anything that Neko had dropped on me. Finding out NiQue was his sister was a lot. His family had always been mixed up in a lot of shit back in the day. Being employed by Darnell Clayton allowed me to see some wild shit, but nothing compared to the shit he had his entire family immersed in.

"Pinky, I can't let anything happen to YaSheema Nicole and I can't let anything happen to Rhina. They're all I have left. If any of the shit the police say is true about YaSheema Nicole and the bouncer from the club, then my wife, who is blindly innocent, could be in danger," Neko said with a serious look on his face. The vein in his forehead thumped and I couldn't help but notice he looked just like his father.

I had never believed in curses or any of that silly shit, but I did believe that the apple doesn't fall too far from the tree. If his niece was anything like he feared, then I guess it was good that I came back from the dead.

Out of the corner of my eye I saw someone come out of the house we had pulled in front of. "Hey, is that her?" I asked as I pointed in the direction of the house.

"Yeah. That's Cassandra," Neko responded, putting his hand on the lever to open the door.

"Naw. You know damn well she ain't gonna talk to you. If she already dropped a dime on your niece to the police, then you know she ain't gonna tell you shit. Let me talk to her," I said, getting out the car before Neko had time to stop me.

I felt my waistband for my gun. I think I was practically itching to use it. I didn't want to hurt the girl, but I did want to get Neko the information he needed; and if I had to scare the girl to get the info, then that's what I was going to do. I quickly walked up the driveway before the young woman had the chance to get to the bottom of the driveway and to her car.

"Excuse me. Cassandra?"

The young girl jumped and looked around. "Yes. What can I do for you?" she asked me. Before she had the chance to move, I lifted my shirt up and showed her the butt of my gun.

"I just need to ask you a few questions, Cassandra. It shouldn't take me more than a few minutes," I grinned. I was slowly, but surely, slipping back into my old ways and it felt good.

"I don't know shit. Just leave me alone," the young girl said, trying to back away from me. I grabbed ahold of her arm and forced her into the back of her car. I kept my hand near my waist and eased to the driver's side and slid into the seat never taking my eyes off of my new friend Cassandra. I turned completely around in the seat and took my gun from my waist and sat it in my lap casually.

"I think you know a lot. Or at least, that's what the cops said. They said you know a lot about your friend YaSheema Nicole. They said you were running your mouth like a fucking bitch! That's what they said. Now we're gonna play a game. I'm gonna ask you a question and you're gonna answer me truthfully. If you don't, I'll shoot you in the fuckin' head. Now how does that sound, Cassandra? Does that sound like a game you wanna play?" I laughed.

The girl shook nervously in the back seat of her car. "Please don't hurt me. I'll tell you everything you want to know. Just don't hurt me," she pleaded.

"Good girl," I smiled. "Now, how did the police know YaSheema Nicole made a threat to that bouncer?" I asked, stroking my gun in my lap as it were a kitten.

"They came to my house talking about they had us

on the club's surveillance cameras having a few words with him. They told me the bouncer was dead and that if I didn't tell them everything that happened I was going to jail with whoever killed him. I swear I just told them the truth. They asked me where I was night before last and I told them how me, YaSheema Nicole, and Vernita hit another club and after I dropped them off, I came straight home. My parents vouched for me. They were up when I got home and that's what they told the cops. I was home when that dude got shot. I ain't have anything to do with any of that. Then the cops starting asking me about YaSheema Nicole; I told them I dropped her off at home and that was that.

"That's all you told them, Cassandra?" I knew she had to tell them more than that for them to be accusing Neko's niece of murder. If I was gonna get the truth out of her, I was gonna have to really scare her. She was scared now, but I wanted that bitch to have nightmares about this moment for the rest of her life. However long that was going to be.

"I think you told them more than that. As a matter of fact, I know you told them more than that. Now I'm going to give you just one more chance to play by the rules before I blow your god damn head off. Now what else did you tell them?" I asked, picking up the gun and pointing it right between her eyes. The young girl pissed her pants and all over her seat she was so petrified. I found the whole ordeal to be funny and burst out laughing at the sight of the telltale peeing in her pants.

"Aight. Aight! I told them that YaSheema Nicole started wildin' out on the bouncer. I told them she threatened him. They asked me if I thought she would really follow through on her threats. I told them I ain't know about that. That was all. I swear that's all I said to them."

Something about her demeanor was off. I knew she was lying and that wasn't all she'd told the cops. My finger caressed the trigger of the gun and I felt a feeling that I hadn't felt in a very long time. It was a mixture of adrenaline and ecstasy. It was the power of holding another human's life in my hands like it was putty. It was what I was really missing. It wasn't just Neko. It was the kill that I missed. It was the fear from my victim that I loved. That's what always made me an effective hit woman.

Cassandra began to cry and I couldn't help but smile at her misery and fear.

"Please lady. I told you everything. Now, please let me go," she pleaded.

"The good thing for you, Cassandra, is that I believe you; but the bad thing is that I don't believe you won't tell on me. And since I don't believe you won't tell on me I have to end this lil' game," I laughed.

Before she could beg for her life, I pulled the trigger, slumping her in the back seat of her car. I sat there admiring how clean I had blown her head off with no regard. I wasn't as rusty as I thought. The only thing that brought me back from my murderous induced high was the sound of tires screeching up next to where the car was parked. Neko was yelling for me to come on. I exited Cassandra's car and got in the car with Neko and he peeled away.

"What the fuck did you do, Pinky? I asked you to talk to her, not shoot her!" Neko yelled as he did his best to maneuver out of the upscale neighborhood without detection.

I pulled the mirror down on the visor on the passenger side of the car and smiled at my reflection. I smiled through the blood spatter on my face from me blowing Cassandra's head clean off her shoulders at close range.

"I did what was needed," I said calmly as I examined my reflection in the mirror. "I got rid of a potential problem for you. She told the police too much and now she can't tell them anything else. If I were you I would start driving I-85 north. I think you'd better find your niece before the police do," I said, never taking my eyes off of my own devious reflection.

Chapter Eighteen

Me and My Bitch
Dread

It is finally Friday and I think I'm starting to get the hang of this working shit. I haven't seen who I thought was my daughter since my first day on the job, but I've been keeping my eye out for her. I have been getting real cozy with Ms. Grey too. In fact, we have plans to go out after work tonight with some of the staff. It was nothing fancy. Just drinks for happy hour. I have to admit, I am looking forward to spending time with Ms. Grey off the clock. She has definitely piqued my curiosity.

We made it through the day and I followed behind Ms. Grey's car to a bar further up Georgia Avenue. When we got inside a few familiar faces from the university were already inside.

"Where do you want to sit? Should we join the others?" I asked Ms. Grey. She shook her head and led me to a private booth.

"I thought it would be better if it were only you and

I," Ms. Grey flirted. Her bold flirting had become more intense as the week had progressed and now it was bubbling over. I could tell Ms. Grey had more interest in me than a work relationship. But I wasn't going to be the one to make the first move. I hadn't been this excited about a woman since YaSheema. Ms. Grey had definitely put me under her spell.

"What are you drinking? This round is on me," she smiled seductively.

"I'll have whatever you're having."

I watched as she signaled for the waitress to come over to our booth. Ms. Grey ordered two Remy 1738s on the rocks and I knew what kind of night it was going to be.

"Ms. Grey..."

"Please call me Tisha. We aren't in the school...you don't have to be so formal. I thought we came here to have fun. Do you know how to have fun, Mr. Evans, or are you always so uptight?"

"I don't think I have had any real fun in a long time, Ms. Gr... I mean...Tisha."

"Well, why don't we have some fun?"

Our conversation, which I'm sure was headed in the wrong direction, was broken up by the waitress bringing our drinks.

"Here's to having fun, Mr. Evans. I think we all need a little every now and again," Tisha said, taking her drink to the head in three long gulps and quickly signaling the waitress to bring us another round.

I knew I should have stopped right there, but I followed along with Tisha Grey's plan and downed my drink too and every drink we ordered thereafter. I don't remember whose idea it was to get on the floor and dance, but I was about ten drinks in the wind now and I didn't remember much. I tried to conceal how turned on Tisha was making me as she bumped and grinded her ass on me song after song. I only stopped her when I had to use the bathroom. It was a good thing too. If she would have jiggled her phat ass on me one more time, I would have bent her over the bar and fucked her like I knew she wanted me to. I would have definitely given our co-workers something to talk about around the water cooler on Monday. I went to the bathroom and handled my business. I washed and dried my hands and right before I grabbed the handle to walk out; in walked Tisha Grey.

"Damn. I was getting lonely out there all by myself," she said in a husky voice.

"I was coming Ms. Grey. Isn't the rest of the staff still out there? You do know you're in the men's room; right?"

"Umm hmm. I know. I am very aware of where we are," she said licking her lips.

"Well, shouldn't we get back out there to the others before they start wondering where we went? I asked, feigning ignorance. I knew what Ms. Grey wanted and I knew why she was there.

"I don't think they're gonna miss us," Tisha said,

locking the door so that no one could come in the men's room and knock what she had planned.

I know the smile that traced along the corners of my mouth probably looked sinister. I was hungry for what Ms. Grey was offering; but if she wanted to keep playing this game, then I would indulge her.

"Well, isn't the party out there?" I asked, playing along with her little game. She moved so close to me that her heaving bosom was pressed against me.

"I think you and I know the real party hasn't even started yet," Ms. Grey moved in and there was no stopping her. Not like I wanted to, but I would prefer not to be engaging in these kinds of acts in a very public restroom.

She didn't respond. She simply smiled and proceeded to rip open my shirt like a mad woman and tugging at my slacks. I know I should have stopped her, but the dog in me wanted her to do whatever she wished; but somehow, her being so aggressive was turning me off. I pushed her off of me and backed her into the sink. I turned her around and bent her over the filthy sink. Lifting her dress up over her thighs, I did what Ms. Grey wanted me to do to her. I fucked her on the sink of the bathroom in the bar like she was a cheap slut and she enjoyed every minute of it. The only thing that stopped our animalistic frenzy was the pounding on the door. There were some angry bar hoppers on the other side of the door who wanted in, when all I finish rocking Tisha's sexy ass to sleep. The pounding of the person on the other side of the door threw me off and all the lust that was there a second ago was gone. Tisha noticed something was wrong and looked back at me. She stood up and turned around and frantically pulled her dress down. Shame danced across her face.

"Oh, my God. I'm so sorry, Mr. Evans. I didn't mean to..." she started to say, but I cut her off.

"Look...I am just as much the blame as you. We both had too many drinks and if we don't get out of here, they're gonna call the cops on us," I said, buttoning my slacks and walking over to the door. Ms. Grey straightened out her clothes and stood behind me. I unlocked the door and let the overweight drunk man that was pounding on the door into the bathroom.

"Sorry man. My wife had too much to drink. She wasn't feeling well and we ran straight in here. We ain't bother to see which bathroom we ran in," I lied.

The drunk staggered past us and wobbled over to a urinal. Ms. Grey walked out with me following close behind. I know all eyes were going to be on us. We had both been gone for over twenty minutes and I am sure someone from the university had noticed we were both missing by now.

We both took a seat and avoided the accusing stares coming from the faculty. After about ten minutes of awkward silence, I decided I had had enough. I told my colleagues that I was going to call it a night. I don't know what made me feel comfy enough to go out with them anyway. I made my way out to my car and it had started to drizzle. I figured that if I hurried, I would be able to catch a liquor store before they all closed and go home with a bottle which was better than any woman in my personal opinion. If nothing else, I could nurse my blue balls with a bottle of liquor.

Just as I slid into the car I heard someone calling my name. "Mr. Evans. Wait up," I heard Ms. Grey calling after me with her heels clicking the ground with every step she took. I took one look at her and decided I was done fucking up my life. I wasn't going to let some woman ruin the little piece of a job I had even if she was the reason I had it in the first place. Me and Ms. Grey fucking around couldn't be anything but trouble and I wanted to stay far away. In fact, I had better things to focus my energy on and it wasn't going to be between this woman's thighs. I had to find out if the young woman I saw a few days ago was my daughter.

"Look...Ms. Grey I think you should get one of your lil' friends in there to drive you home. That's what I'm gonna do. Go home and I am going home alone. I think we have done enough damage for one evening. We don't need our working relationship to get weird because we couldn't control our hormones."

"Ronald I know I am a lil' tipsy, but what happened back there was going to happen if I was sober or drunk. I am attracted to you and I think you are attracted to me too. Why can't we be two adults about this and stop dancing around how we feel? I like you, Mr. Evans and I think somewhere deep down you like me too."

I looked at Ms. Grey as the rain started to come down harder. Her mascara started to run down her cheeks as the rain went from drizzle to a downpour. She had no idea that I was exactly what she didn't need. My history and track record with women wasn't good at all. That's probably why I had taken to doing the one night stand thing so I would never have to deal with the women afterwards. All these years of screwing up relationship after relationship or running into the wrong women was going to be the death of me.

I had fucked up with YaSheema. Then I screwed up fucking with NiQue, and having sex with that stripper bitch, Pinky, almost cost me my life. Then to top it all off, I left my daughter. Now here I was having a soft side for a woman that was responsible for the job I now have. I owed Ms. Grey much more that I could offer her and I knew I would end up nothing but a disappointment to her later.

"Ms. Grey, I don't think you need or want a nigga like me in your life. It might be best for us to keep things on a business level between us. I don't want things to get out of control. Maybe you should go on home because that's what I'm going to do. It ain't what I want to do, but it's what I need to do for the both of us. Have a good night and weekend, Ms. Grey," I said and pulled my door closed before my interior got too wet from the rain.

I pulled my seatbelt on and noticed Ms. Grey

hadn't budged. She was still standing there in the rain looking through my car window like she couldn't believe I had turned her down. If she only knew that I was doing what I thought was best for the both of us. I wasn't what she deserved and I didn't want to treat her like the women I had done wrong in the past. She was better than a wham bam thank you ma'am.

Finally Ms. Grey walked away and got in her own car and I pulled off. The only bitch I needed in my life was a bottle. She was the best kind of bitch too. I didn't catch feelings and she always fucked me right. Yeah, the bottle was the only thing I needed. I ain't have nothing else.

Chapter Nineteen

Neko Reynolds
Old Friends and the Usual Suspects

I've been locked in my room for days worried sick about my wife and niece. Neither of them are answering their phones. I only calmed down when I called Howard University and was able to confirm that YaSheema Nicole had checked in. That eased my mind some. At least she had made it to school. I know me and my niece parted on bad terms, but she's never pulled anything like this. Not to mention, Rhina still hasn't surfaced. She still hasn't called to tell me she made it to D.C. and after Pinky killed Cassandra, I don't want anything to do with the police. Even if I called the police to file a missing person's report, they probably wouldn't bother to help me find her. They were too busy looking for YaSheema Nicole themselves. The only offer of help I had was Pinky and she pissed me off for killing Cassandra in cold blood. I sent her packing back to D.C. I know she meant well, but I wasn't used to that kind of shit anymore. I left that life behind when I buried my sisters. Besides, that girl didn't deserve to die, even if she was a snitch.

Now I was sitting in my house alone and wondering what to do next. I figured I would drive to D.C. since YaSheema Nicole had checked in at school. My cell phone rang and I jumped up to find it on the bed. The familiar name flash across the screen made me hopeful about my situation.

"Shadow...my nigga! Wassup with you?"

"What's good you ole cat-eyed nigga. I ain't heard from your ole pretty ass in about six months. I thought you forgot about ya boy," Shadow chuckled. "I got your text and I'm hitting you back. What cha need?" he asked.

"Sorry about not hitting you up sooner. Shit has been kinda' crazy. My niece graduated from high school and got accepted at Howard. Rhina and I have been busy getting her ready for her move up north. Look... that's what I want to talk to you about. I need to come up there and crash for a minute. Rhina is missing, but YaSheema Nicole checked in at school; I ain't heard anything from either of them since the night they left for D.C." I paused and waited to make sure Shadow was listening. I needed him to understand what I was saying to him.

"Damn, my nigga. They probably just got to Drama City and started partying. Ain't your wife from up here anyway? She's probably at her people's spot and just forgot to call you," Shadow tried to reassure me.

"Naw. I think something else may have happened, but I ain't sure. Not hearing from them for a week got me uptight and I can't take it no mo'. I'm gonna get some rest then drive up and check on my niece. She checked in to school, so I guess I will start with her and then I will check with Rhina's family. My nigga that ain't the craziest shit that's happened either. You will never guess who came all the way to Atlanta to find me."

"Who?"

"Pinky," I said. Then I paused because Shadow knew just like I thought I knew, Pinky was supposed to be dead and buried. He was one of my oldest friends. He was there when the police told me she died. I could tell by his gasp followed by silence that he was as shocked as I was.

"You don't mean shawty from way back with the pink hair; do you? How the fuck could that be? Didn't shawty die in a motorcycle accident? How the fuck did she find you?" Shadow asked.

"Shadow, she showed up on my front porch in Georgia a few days back. As a matter of fact, she showed up the same day my niece and wife went missing. I don't know if the shit is connected, but I need to find out. You know Pink was always on some different shit back then, and from what she showed me while she was here, she ain't changed," I explained, careful to choose my words wisely. I didn't want to say the wrong thing or accuse Pinky of something and all of this was just coincidental.

"Well, where is Pinky now? Is she still in Georgia with you?"

"Naw, I sent her back to D.C. Shit was getting weird and her showing up when she did fucked my head up. Now I am gonna close up shop down here for a few days to come to D.C. I need to find out what the fuck is going on. I'm gonna need somewhere to lay my head. I would stay in a hotel, but if something janky is going on, I don't want to use my credit cards. You understand?"

"Yeah, I got you nigga. Just let me know when you get in town. I got you. I'm in the same spot. Do you need the address or do you remember where I'm at?" Shadow asked.

"I know you ain't telling me you are still living in the hood, Shadow. I left you the shop and everything when I moved down here. You should be rolling in the dough by now."

"Ain't no dough rolling when you got all these kids like I got. All of their asses smart too, Neko. I'm paying for all seven of their asses to go to college," Shadow laughed.

Shadow had seven children and if you let him off of his leash he would probably make seven more. He was a ladies man before I moved to Georgia; and knowing him like I did, I was willing to bet he was a ladies' man now.

"I bet you won't have another one," I chuckled.

"Hell, naw nigga! My baby making days are over. They have been over for some time now. Look...hit me up when you cross the city limits. I'll have the place ready for you when you touch down."

I said my goodbyes to Shadow and then Pinky crossed my mind again. A thought popped in my head and I don't know why I hadn't thought about it before. I picked up my cell phone and hoped she wouldn't just hang up on me when I called. She answered on the first ring and I swallowed the lump in my throat. I knew I was wrong as two left shoes for asking her for anything considering I had basically told her to get out of my life after she had smoked Cassandra.

"Pinky, it's me Neko. I know we parted on bad terms and I wanted to apologize. It turns out that I will be headed up north after all. I was wondering if you could do me a huge favor before I get there."

"Umm hmm. What do you need, Neko?" she sighed into the phone.

"I need you to make sure YaSheema Nicole is in school like she's supposed to be. I thought since you worked at the school you could confirm that she was really there. Could you look around and see if you see her for me?"

"Oh, now you need my help? I haven't been back to work since I left Atlanta. I am not due back in the office until Monday and being that it's Friday I don't know how much help I'm going to be. I'll tell you what...when I get to work on Monday, I will check the registry and see if she checked in. If you need me to, I will go to her dorm and make sure she's there. Then I'll call you back."

"Pinky, I know I don't have to tell you this, but be careful and please don't let her know I am coming up there. Whatever you do, do not let her know I sent you to look in on her," I warned Pinky.

"Yeah, whatever Neko. I will let you know what I find out on Monday when I get to work. When will you be here anyway?"

"I should be there on Tuesday or Wednesday. Look…thanks again Pinky. I owe you big time for this." Then I hung up.

I hated lying to Pinky. I didn't need anyone to know when I would be arriving in town. My family still has enemies in Drama City and I damn sure didn't want to alert anyone of my arrival. That included Pinky. I mean…she knew I was coming, but she had no idea I was preparing myself to leave tonight and she didn't need to know that either.

Chapter Twenty

Unleashing the Beast
YaSheema Nicole

I've been on campus for a whole week and I am excited to say that I think I'm going to like it here. Coming to D.C. was the best decision I think I could have made for myself. I even made an effort to get to know my roomie Paige. I found out she is in her second year here at Howard and she isn't as goofy as I initially thought she was. Takiya still doesn't like her though. She doesn't like anyone. Sometimes I don't think she likes me either.

Takiya has been quiet for the last couple of days since I moved on campus and I am grateful. The only noise she's made was when she had me use Aunt Rhina's credit card from her wallet to continue paying for the hotel room I left Rhina's body in in Richmond. Takiya said that if we kept paying for the room, no one would bother the room and find out that Rhina was in there. By then, my alibi would have been established. To say Takiya thought about everything was an understatement. She was always a step ahead and I was always struggling to keep up. Takiya was always making my life difficult, but she was making good on her promises to take care of everything.

Now it was Friday and I had been chatting with Lamont on Facetime and I finally agreed to go out with him. Takiya was totally against that. When she found out I was going to go out with him, she did everything to keep me from going. I guess she didn't know what it was like to be lonely. She always had me, so I guess she was never really alone. I, on the other hand, needed some interaction with the outside world. I still hadn't spoken with Uncle Neko. It ain't because I didn't want to talk to him. It's because I didn't know what to say to him. I had let his wife die alone in a hotel room out of state and I didn't even bother to do anything about it.

You shouldn't feel guilty about that. We probably did her whack ass a favor by killing her.

I ignored Takiya and started getting myself ready for my date with Lamont. The fall weather in D.C. was much cooler than what I was used to, so I decided to wear a simple pair of jeans and a nice blouse. I studied myself hoping I wasn't underdressed for whatever Lamont had planned. I was so excited about him asking me out that I didn't bother to ask him where we were going.

At seven, Paige came in with a bunch of her friends and she invited me to a campus party. I told her I was going out and that she should leave me the address to where the party was so I could stop through if my plans changed. She scribbled the address down on a notepad and left it on my desk and left. About ten minutes after she left, Lamont called my phone and asked me if I was ready. I told him I was and he told me he was in the lobby of the dorm.

When I got downstairs, Lamont was leaning on one of the bookshelves with his shades on. I couldn't understand why he had them on being that it was early evening, but I didn't question it. He was standing there looking as scrumptious as the day I met him. He had a fresh shape up and his clothes were flawless. When he caught sight of me he smiled from ear to ear.

I returned the smile and closed the distance between us.

I don't think you should go out with this joker. Something about him ain't right. You watch what I tell you. He's gonna be a problem. I can feel it. He ain't the reason we're in D.C. We're supposed to be finding your father not finding niggas to lie up with. Takiya whispered inside of my head, making me uncomfortable. She always found the worst possible times to barge in. I shrugged her off and greeted Lamont.

"Hi. You didn't say where we were going so I didn't know what to wear," I said shyly.

"Naw, baby girl, you're perfect. We're just gonna head to Georgetown and see if we can catch a movie and grab something to eat. I figured since you ain't from around here, I could be your private tour guide," he said, licking his lips.

"Well, let's go then," I said excited about spending time with him.

We went to the movies and caught some flick that was playing. I don't even remember what the movie was about because Lamont and I spent the majority of the movie talking and exchanging glances. Once the movie was over, we strolled through historic Georgetown hand in hand. We passed by many clothing shops and bars that were lit up even at that hour of the night. I had never seen anything like Georgetown before and I was mesmerized by the people and its beauty. My Uncle Neko had spoken of living here briefly and it was everything he had claimed it to be.

Lamont pointed out different landmarks and led me around until we both decided to grab something to eat. He said he was going to take me to a spot in Northeast that supposedly had the best fish in the city. We pulled up in front of a little hole in the wall called Horace and Dickies. It sat on a side street from the posh H Street in Northeast D.C. The fish joint had no tables and you called out your order to one lady and another tired looking woman took your money. The counter held makeshift tip jars made out of old Lemon Head candy containers. The entire establishment, if you could call it that, was suspect; but the line of hungry customers told me otherwise. I liked different stuff; but I didn't think this place had anything I wanted, but I didn't want to seem rude. We ordered two fish sandwiches and lemonade. I watched as the cook opened a loaf of bread and laid sizzling hot fish from grease that had to be two months old on it.

"So, tell me about yourself, YaSheema. Why did you come to D.C.to go to school with so many good schools in the south? I would have expected you to stay in the Bible Belt. You don't seem like you belong here. Why Howard? Do you know anyone here?" Lamont asked while we waited for our order.

"I needed to get out of Atlanta. I spent the majority of my life there and it was time to get out of there. I am originally from D.C. I was born here, but I was raised in Georgia. My uncle moved us out of D.C. when I was about one. I really don't know much about D.C. but that's what college is about; right? New experiences?" I responded. I didn't know him well enough to tell him the real reason I was here. Sure I wanted to get a good education, but the other reason for being in D.C. was none of his business yet.

The woman at the counter called our number and we got our food and got back in the car. To my surprise, the sandwich was better than I thought it would be. Lamont spent the rest of the night being my private tour guide of Washington, D.C. I never imagined that the capital city would have areas that were crime ridden and drug infested. Lamont pulled up in a park and I started feeling nervous. He killed the engine and turned off the lights in a secluded part of the park's many parking lots. The sun had gone down hours ago and I didn't know if being that close to him so fast was a good idea.

"Umm, why did we come here? I don't think being in a park after dark is a good idea," I said, scanning the area. I instantly started to panic and look for places to run if I had to.

"Damn...chill, YaSheema. I got you baby. Ain't nothing gonna happen that you don't want to happen. I don't get down like that. If you ain't with anything more than talking, then I'm cool with that. You ain't gotta be afraid of me," Lamont said.

Don't trust this nigga. He could be a rapist. I already told you that I ain't trust his ass. I don't know what it is about his fuck boy ass, but he can't be this nice for no reason. You need to make him take us home. Takiya demanded. I hated when she played off of my emotions.

"Lamont, I think it's best if you take me back to my dorm. I don't think being here is a good idea right now," I said. Maybe Takiya was right about him.

"I told you I ain't gonna do nothing to you, but if you want to act all shitty then I'll take you home," Lamont said firmly. He backed out of the space and sped out of the parking lot and we rode in silence for about ten minutes before I started noticing the scenery was becoming more rural. I had only been in D.C. for a week, so I didn't venture too far from campus, but nothing looked familiar. I tried desperately to get a glimpse of a street sign, but this nigga was speeding down narrow two lane roads that no one should speed through.

I thought about opening the door and jumping out. We were going sixty miles per hour and jumping out wasn't going to be a smart thing to do if I wanted to live. I was going to have to wait until he stopped the car and make a run for it as soon as he stopped the car. I was all prepared to run when he pulled into an old trailer park. As soon as he stopped the car, I pulled the latch to open the car door, but Lamont was too fast. He reached out and grabbed a fistful of my hair pulling me toward him. My back violently slammed into the gear shift causing me to wince in pain.

"Ahh!" I cried out in pain.

"Bitch, I wasn't trying to do nothing but talk to your stuck up country ass. Now since you didn't want to let me be a gentleman and show you a good time the right way; I guess I'm gonna have to do it the wrong way," Lamont growled, snatching me around wildly and causing me to hit my head on the steering wheel.

"Please don't hurt me," I begged, but my pleas fell on deaf ears. Lamont held me in place by my hair with my head wedged between the steering wheel and his lap.

"Hold still and shut the fuck up, bitch. I'ma give you something to remember about the DMV!" Lamont yelled, gripping my hair tighter. He fumbled with his free hand down by his door and when his free hand came back into my view he had a switchblade in his hand and all the fight I had was gone. Either I had better do what he said or he might kill me.

Lamont yanked my head again and put the knife up to my throat. "Take off those jeans. If you ain't want this dick why did you go out with me? You ain't shit but a tease. Now this is what you're gonna do. You're gonna unfasten your pants and pull down your panties. If you try to make a move other than pulling your pants down I will cut you! You got that?"

I did what he said and pulled my pants down as best as I could with him holding the knife to my throat. I couldn't believe this was happening to me. Where was Takiya now and why wasn't she helping me? I was able to get my pants down a little past my thighs. Being in the awkward position and held at knifepoint prevented me from getting them down any further. Apparently that was all Lamont needed. He put the knife on the dashboard and his hands violated me in the worst way. He ripped my blouse open and pawed at my breast. I cringed from his touch and he slapped me so hard all I could see was a bright light flash before me like the flash from a camera.

"Didn't I tell you not to move? You're gonna make me kill you!" he said with his hands travelling down below my waistline and into my womanhood. I cried out. My body wasn't aroused so his finger's entry was unwelcomed. After he got frustrated because my body wouldn't respond to him, he opened his door and grabbed the knife off the dash. He dragged me out like I was a weightless ragdoll and threw me to the ground. I couldn't run because my pants were tangled. My bare ass was on the concrete and he proceeded to drag me to the back of the car. He opened the backdoor and made me get inside.

"Lay on your back bitch," he growled.

I did as he instructed. If I didn't...he would kill me. Lamont pulled my slides off of my feet and my jeans off. He unfastened his pants and climbed on top of me with his hand wrapped around the handle of the knife. I lay perfectly still while Lamont raped me over and over again in the back of his car in a trailer park. When he was done, he tossed me out of the car and spit on me.

"Don't even think of telling anyone shit. It ain't like they're gonna believe your slow country ass anyway," Lamont laughed as he pulled his pants up and got back in his car. I didn't move because if I did there was no telling what his crazy ass would do.

"Bitch count to one hundred and then you can get up," he barked then he cranked up the engine, made U-turn and sped off into the night. As soon as I couldn't see his tail lights anymore, I got up on my feet as quickly as I could. My insides ached from the brutal attack, but I had to get out of there in case Lamont decided to not be so generous and come back and finish me off.

My eyes searched all around and they landed on a

trailer that had all of the interior lights on. There was no shame in my game. I hobbled over to the trailer and banged on the door for dear life. I just hoped that the people on the other side would take pity on me and help me. When the door of the trailer opened, a little old white lady peered out at me in horror.

"Oh, my God! Chile, what done up and happened to you?"

I looked down at myself and I hadn't noticed before that I was still naked from the waist down with Lamont's semen running down my thighs and my blouse was wide open. All I could think about was getting away from where Lamont had left me.

"Dear God, chile. What the Sam hell happened to you?" the woman asked with a wide-eyed stare plastered across her face.

Just as I was about to tell the woman what happened, I saw headlights headed in our direction and my fear returned full force.

"Ma'am, please...can you just let me in before he comes back? If he sees me talking to you he will come after me," I cried hysterically. The woman moved aside and let me in. She told me to wait right there while she went to the back to find something for me to put on. As soon as the woman was out of my sight Takiya popped up.

Now will you listen to me when I tell you I don't trust someone?

"You left me, Takiya. He could have killed me and

you didn't do anything to stop him," I whispered. I didn't want to startle the woman who was kind enough to let me into her home and help me.

I had to teach you a lesson first. You had to learn that what I say does matter. I just don't tell you shit to hear myself talk. I told you that fuck nigga was shady and you ain't believe me. You still went out with him and look where that got you. That got your gullible ass raped, naked and stranded in God only knows where.

I felt the hot tears pouring from my eyes while I stood there naked and shivering. I didn't need to be chastised at a time like this. I needed help and Takiya was pressed to hear that she was right about Lamont and how wrong I was about him.

"Look, Takiya you were right and I was wrong. Is that what you wanted to hear? I was wrong! Now what are we gonna do about it? This poor lady is probably scared out of her mind back there. She might even be calling the cops as we speak. So since you have all the bright ideas...what the fuck do you want me to do?" I damn near screamed.

Takiya laughed and then proceeded to tell me what she wanted me to do. *I want you to get the clothes from the old hag. Make sure she doesn't call the police and see if you can get her to take you back to the campus. After you get back to the dorm, I will take it from there. Can you handle that or do you need me to write it down for you?* Takiya chuckled, but I was far from amused. I had been beaten, raped and left naked in the middle of nowhere and this bitch thought it was funny. I sucked my teeth and rolled my eyes.

When the little old lady came out from the back, she was carrying a pair of jogging pants and a sweatshirt that had seen better days. I didn't complain though. I politely took the items from her and she pointed me to a bathroom. When I returned, the woman was sitting on her couch with a grim look on her face.

"Baby, maybe you should call the police. There's no telling what that man will do to you next," she said, getting up and heading in the direction of the phone.

"No! No police. He said if I called the police he will kill me. He knows where I live and if I call the cops on him he'll come after me," I said, refusing the phone she was trying to offer me.

"Well, what are you gonna do? You certainly can't stay here and if you let that wild dog run free there's no telling how many other women he will have his way with," she said stunned.

"Ma'am, I just want to go home. If you could do me the favor of taking me home I would greatly appreciate it."

"Well, where is home baby, because I normally don't drive after the sun goes down for reasons just like yours. I don't wanna end up a victim," the woman said a bit too sarcastic for my liking.

"I'm a student at Howard University and I live on campus," I said, hoping the woman had an ounce of compassion for me.

"That's about thirty minutes out of the way. Not to mention, I would have to drive all the way back home by myself," she gasped.

"Ma'am, I hate to take you out of your way, but I wouldn't ask if I didn't need it. I have money and I will gladly give you everything I have in my room if you'll just take me home," I pleaded.

Why are you begging that old bag for anything? If we need her fuckin' car, take her God damn car! She's like two seconds from death. Knock her old ass out, find the keys and get us out of here! Oh fuck it, I will do it myself. I gotta do everything else for you anyway. Next I'll be helping you wipe your ass!

"No! I'm not gonna hit that old woman!" I screamed, frustrated with Takiya. I covered both of my ears and shook my head back and forth to drown out the sound of Takiya's voice. The old lady looked at me and I could read the fear written on her face. She knew she had made a grave mistake opening the door to help me.

"Look here missy, maybe you should just leave. If you don't get out of here, I'm gonna call the cops on you," the scared white lady said, backing away from me, but it was too late. Takiya saw a way out and she was going to take it.

My steps were no longer my own as Takiya took control. The last thing I remember is walking toward the old lady and putting my hands around her slender, pale neck and everything else after that was a blur.

Chapter Twenty-One

Old Habits Die Hard
Pinky York

It was early Saturday morning and I didn't sleep a wink last night. I think the anticipation of Neko coming to D.C. had me on edge. No matter how hard I tried to get him out of my system, the harder it became to let him go. Now he wants me to check up on his niece. What I should have said was 'no' but instead, I told him I would.

I got up and cleaned myself up and turned on the news while I made a pot of coffee and twisted up a blunt. I sat there contemplating if I should really help Neko or not when there was a breaking report that flashed across the screen.

This is Giovanni Drummond with News Channel 8. I'm on site of a blazing fire at Flower Village Mobile Home Park in Upper Marlboro, Maryland. What we were able to find out is that the trailer belonged to an elderly widow; a Mrs. Catherine Kramer who was eighty-three years old who perished in the fire.

The bizarre twist in this ongoing investigation is that police sources believe that the fire behind me was to cover up a brutal homicide. If anyone was in the area of this mobile park between midnight and six this morning, you are asked to contact the authorities.

Also, Mrs. Kramer's neighbors reported seeing an unidentified vehicle leaving the area around midnight and Mrs. Kramer's 1990 Lincoln Town Car is missing. Again, if you have any information you are urged to contact Crime Solvers at 301-555-1212. Your information will remain anonymous.

I sat there watching the news in horror. Who would kill an eighty-three-year-old woman? Either she was mixed up in some bad shit or she was just a victim. Either way, it was fucked up.

I finished my coffee and decided to do what I knew I shouldn't do. I got dressed and went to my office. I needed to find out all I could on Neko's niece and make sure her lil' ass was where she was supposed to be before he got to town.

When I got to the campus and the administrative offices, I was grateful that it was a Saturday morning and no one was really around to get on my nerves. I didn't feel like hearing my boss ask me a million and one questions about my absence for an entire week. When I got to my office, the first thing I noticed was the stack of work waiting for me. I can't say I was excited about what I was going to have to do come Monday morning. I hated working. I pushed the papers to the side, sat down in front of my computer and logged into the university's student roster. I pulled up YaSheema Nicole's file and jotted down her room assignment so I could check to make sure she was really there. From the looks of everything in my computer, she had checked in earlier this week. I guess Neko didn't have anything to worry about. His precious niece was safe and sound.

I swiveled in my chair and knocked over the stack of papers that was looming about my desk onto the floor. I mumbled a few choice words before picking the paper up. That's when, for the second time in under a month, I almost had the wind knocked out of me. The name Ronald Evans stood out like a sore thumb. I picked the paper up and examined it. My luck couldn't be this damn good. I inspected the paper as though it were foreign and found out it was the Ronald "Dread" Evans I had almost killed. This was the man I believe killed my sister outside of a D.C. nightclub seventeen years ago. He was the same one I shot and left for dead; but to my surprise, he hadn't died and now I was holding info for his campus access badge. He was now a part of the H.U. staff and I was the one who had to grant him his permissions to access certain places on campus.

I smiled because I couldn't believe my luck. What were the odds of me and ole boy Dread working in the same place? I assigned his badge and put it in his mailbox in the main office. I didn't want to hand it to him personally like I normally did. I wasn't ready for

Mr. Evans and I to become reacquainted just yet. I had to prepare for our meeting because it was going to be explosive.

Now that I had programed his keycard, I could keep tabs on him at all times via the school's monitoring system. When the time was right, I was going to make him wish I had killed his bitch ass the first time. After digging up as much dirt as I could on Dread through his files, I strolled over to the dorm to check on YaSheema. Then it hit me. YaSheema Nicole was Dread's daughter. I definitely couldn't let her know I knew him.

I pulled my jacket around me as the autumn wind whipped all around me. I took a few more steps and bent the corner and my heart began to beat wildly in my chest. There were police all over the faculty parking lot and there were crime scene investigators roping off the area. I walked up to the crowd that had gathered around the area behind the yellow crime scene tape.

"What happened?" I asked one of the onlookers.

"Someone said they found a car that has something to do with an old lady in Upper Marlboro that they found dead. I guess whoever torched the old broad took her car and left it here and ran. Damn shame," the informant said.

I looked around and saw the news trucks and reporters preparing to break the news first. I shook my head and walked around the outside of the crime scene and over to the dorm. Once inside, I was checked in at the front desk by one of the assistant resident managers, Alma. She and I chatted about what was happening in the parking lot for a few minutes and then I went to YaSheema Nicole's floor. I knocked lightly on her door and heard some shuffling.

"Who is it?"

"Ahh, my name is Ms. York and I was just checking to make sure you had settled in ok," I lied. I hope she bought that bullshit because I wouldn't have. To my surprise, I heard the locks on the door slide from their chambers and the door opened.

Even though I had seen pictures of YaSheema Nicole and I had seen her in our chance passing in Georgia, her resemblance to her aunt was amazing. YaSheema looked eerily like YaYa Clayton. So much so, it sent a shiver up my spine. Her stormy grey eyes looked exactly like that of my late employer's daughter and Neko's. The only difference was she was a half of a shade lighter than YaYa and she had dirty reddish hair like Dread.

I swallowed hard and tried not to stare at her.

"I'm settled in just fine. Thank you for checking. Is there anything else?" she said a little too snotty for me, but I had to hold my composure. I didn't need to have a confrontation with her. I just needed to make sure she was definitely here to calm Neko down and then hopefully get her to lead me to her father.

"That's all, Ms. Evans. Just checking to make sure you're all settled in and ready for classes."

YaSheema Nicole tilted her head like she was

studying me and then she smiled. It wasn't a friendly smile either. It was sort of sick. "I'm good. You know... you look awfully familiar. Have we met?" she asked.

The smile on her face gave me the creeps. I had done some ill shit in my day and nothing really fazed me, but I had to admit this young girl had me shook. Something about the way she was looking at me made me feel like she had me all figured out. I have never felt like this before.

"Umm, I don't think so. I'm just a part of the campus welcome committee...just doing my job. That's all," I said nervously, but impressed by the way I lied with a straight face.

"Well, ok. Thanks for checking, Ms. York. Have a good afternoon," she said and started to close the door then she stopped and swung it back open. "Ms. York... why didn't you ask how Paige is? If you're the welcome committee, I'm sure you know I ain't the only one in this room. Why ain't you ask about my roomie?" she asked, still smiling that sick, demented smile.

"I only had your name to check on. I'm sure someone will be by to check on Paige," I stuttered.

"Umm hmm. Have a good weekend, Ms. York." YaSheema Nicole said and slammed the door in my face. I was glad she did. I didn't want to do anything but get the fuck out of there. I hated to admit it, but that bitch had me shook. I knew YaSheema Nicole and I were going to cross paths again and I wasn't so sure if I wanted to.

Chapter Twenty-Two

Welcome to the District
Neko Reynolds

As soon as I saw the first sign that welcomed me to Washington, D.C., I knew I didn't belong here. This was no longer my home and she didn't love me like she used to. Although I had to come to D.C. to find my wife and niece, I wasn't excited to be here.

I crossed the Woodrow Wilson Bridge and peered into the murky waters of the Potomac. The Potomac River – or the Anacostia as native Washingtonians liked to call it – was the source of some of misery. My sister and best friend YaYa, and my mother, had both been found dead in the Anacostia. Memories of my sister flooded my mind and I smiled. She was the best thing that had ever happened to me despite all the things that came along with being her brother. I loved YaSheema Clayton.

I stepped on the gas and thought about all the things I left behind in D.C. Reminiscing made me remember to call Shadow to let him know I had touched down. It had been seventeen years since I had been back home, but I remembered my way through the city. I navigated through what used to be the hood that was now gentrified. Places that were notoriously dangerous back in the day were now cleaned up and livable.

Looking at Southeast D.C. now one would never know it was drug infested and that my family owned this portion of the city. My father and sister ruled over the Southside by pumping drugs through the hood with the help of some of their most trusted employees. One of which was my former girlfriend, Pinky York, who had returned from the dead to profess her undying love for me.

Thinking of Pinky made me shake my head. There was no doubt that I still loved her. She was my ghetto love and no one could replace her. Not even Rhina with her degrees and her private practice could compare to the excitement of Pinky. Pinky was wild and free. There was no taming her and she never tried to tame me either. Maybe that's why we had always gotten along so well in the past. She did her and I did me. There was no in between.

Pinky allowed me to be me. She never pushed for more than what we were. We loved each other and we loved hard. The only problem Pink and I had was that I couldn't keep my dick in my pants and she turned cold when her sister died. I still never got all of the details about the night her sister died. I was only able to find out that Detective Gatsby was the one who murdered Pinky's sister. Pinky thought Dread had something to do with her sister's death, and I could never figure out why she assumed that. Dread was many things, but a killer he was not.

I pulled up in front of Shadow's apartment and couldn't believe my nigga still lived in the same place after all these years. You would have thought with time he would have upgraded himself; but like he said, with all the kids he has, how could he?

I killed the engine and stepped out the car feeling strange to be back in the capital city. I watched in amazement as some youth walked down the sidewalk passing a blunt back and forth like it was nothing. Then I remembered they had decriminalized weed here a few years back. That was never going to fly in the south.

I walked to the building that I remembered as Shadow's and used the intercom to let him know I was here...I was home. Shadow buzzed me in and I climbed the steps to his apartment. Just as I was about to knock on his door, the door flew open and Shadow was standing there with a grin as big as the state of Texas on his face.

"My nigga...what it do? Man, oh man it's been far too long," Shadow said hugging me.

"Yeah, I know. I'ma try to get up here more often," I said, walking inside. To my surprise, his apartment was neatly decked out. Pictures of all of his children lined the walls and there was even a picture of Shadow and I from when I opened the detailing shop. He lived in the same place, but it was much neater than when we used to hang years ago.

"That was a long time ago; huh man?" Shadow said as he observed me looking at the photo.

"Yeah. It feels like it was centuries ago," I said. Then I came across a framed picture of me, Shadow and NiQue. Seeing the picture of my sister made my blood run cold and it reminded me of what I was doing here in the first place. I took a seat on the couch and attempted to get comfortable but the big elephant in the room was preventing that. Shadow took a seat across from me and I knew it was coming.

"I thought you said you would never come back to D.C. And what's up with Pinky coming back from the dead? I thought ole girl got 187'd before you decided to leave here?"

"I thought she was dead too. She just showed up on my porch a few days ago. Shit ain't sitting right. I know this may sound crazy, but I don't think it's a coincidence that she showed up right now. Now Rhina is M.I.A. and YaSheema Nicole hasn't returned any of my calls either. That ain't like either of them to ignore my calls. I called Pinky before I got on the road up here to see if she would be able to get me any information on my niece's whereabouts. I lied to her and told her that I wouldn't be here until Monday or Tuesday. No one knows I'm in the city but you and I wanna keep it that way. You feel me?"

"Nigga, that's some heavy shit. Let me ask you this... have you heard from your niece's father? I know you and ole boy weren't on the best of terms, but I think maybe you should give him a heads up that his seed is in town. You don't want them running into each other unexpectedly. That shit could get ugly," Shadow said, breaking down a big bud of weed on a magazine.

"I thought about calling him and telling him that she was here, but what am I supposed to say to him? He ain't want anything to do with the girl. Why would he give a fuck about her now? Besides, I don't even know if that nigga is still in the area or not. The last time I had contact with him was a few years ago when I sent him pictures of YaSheema Nicole. My niece, on the other hand, is very interested in her father. She's been asking me over and over again for years about him. I ain't know what to tell her about him. What was I supposed to say...your father didn't want you because your mother and aunt drove that nigga crazy?"

Shadow shrugged and continued rolling his blunt. Then he stopped what he was doing and looked at me like a light bulb went off inside his head. "My daughter Paige is in her second year at Howard. Her mother and step-father checked her in last weekend. Maybe I could call her and see if she has seen your peoples around. I know it's a long shot being that Howard is huge, but it won't hurt to ask," Shadow said, passing me the rolled blunt.

I lit the blunt and nodded my head at Shadow. "Make sure you keep it on the low that I'm looking for my niece. I don't wanna tip her off that I'm in town. There's something else Shadow," I said passing him the blunt.

"What's that?"

"You remember how my sister NiQue was a lil' off before she died?'

"A lil' off? Shawty was all the way gone. She tried to burn down the shop and kill you and her own baby. That bitch was crazy!" Shadow said between taking pulls from the blunt. "Aww, damn man...no disrespect intended. I know that was your family," Shadow said after realizing I wasn't feeling him talking about my sister like that. I know NiQue was crazy as bat shit, but she was still my sister. NiQue needed help, love and guidance. She never got it and that caused her illness to spiral out of control until it took over her. It wasn't her fault she was fucked up.

"I know NiQue had some issues. It wasn't her fault though. My pops treated her like she was an outcast instead of getting her the medical attention she needed. It fucked her up completely to watch my father dote on YaYa and then take me in without ever having a relationship with her. NiQue was screwed up because my father didn't want anything to do with her and I think NiQue passed on her illness to YaSheema Nicole."

Shadow dropped the lit blunt in his lap out of shock.

"Nigga, you ain't telling me niecy got the same shit are you?" Shadow said, trying to pick up the blunt before it burned a hole in the chair.

"I don't know, Shadow. I really don't know. I mean...all of the signs are there. I've been trying to ignore them, but I would catch YaSheema Nicole talking to herself and her moods would change like the blowing of the wind," I said, taking the blunt as he passed it my way.

"Then there is the matter of the police showing up at my crib the day after she left to come up here. They wanted to question her in connection with a murder in Georgia."

"Man! Your peoples always got something going on. Why would the police think your niece got something to do with a murder?" Shadow asked.

"Her friend told the cops they should question YaSheema Nicole about the murder because she made some threats to the dude the night he was killed. Several people heard YaSheema make the threats, so the police think she really followed through with them. Now I can't get her to return my calls. Shadow, this shit is all fucked up and I don't know where to start. I feel like I am going backwards in time. I feel like I have been dropped seventeen years in the past; aint shit adding up. Niggas popping up that were supposed to be dead and my niece ain't returning calls and I think Rhina is missing. I hate to think the worst, but with my family history, there's no telling what's going on."

"I sure hope you ain't got problems like you had in the past; because if you do, you're fucked!" Shadow choked on the blunt.

I sat there thinking about everything and Shadow was right. If I was reliving the past it may not play out so sweet this time and I wasn't ready to see how it all was going to end. I slipped into my own private thoughts while Shadow made a call to his daughter, Paige. He left her a message and as he hung up, my cell phone rang in my pocket.

Pinky's name flashed across the screen and I answered before it rang for the second time.

"Hello."

"Yeah, Neko your niece is safe and sound on campus. According to the school system, she's been here for a few days. I'll keep an eye on her till you get here," Pinky offered.

"Thanks, Pinky. I appreciate you taking the time to check on her for me. I'll see you in a couple days when I get to the city," I said

"Ok, Neko and you're welcome," she said and then she hung up.

Once I put my phone away I noticed Shadow was staring at me.

"What nigga?" I asked him.

"You better be careful my nigga. You might be fucking around with fire fucking with Pinky again. You're a married man now and females like Pinky are detrimental to a marriage. That's exactly why I ain't never getting married," he laughed.

I chuckled at his half-witted humor, but I knew he was right. Getting caught up slipping with Pinky could fuck up my happy home that I had worked so hard to build. However, something deep down told me that there was no way to avoid Pinky and I really don't think I really wanted to.

Chapter Twenty-Three

Dread

I woke up to the sound of my iPhone chirping. I checked the time and was shocked to see it was midday. I had slept most of my Saturday away. I guess that bottle I picked up after parting ways with Ms. Grey was to blame. I answered my phone and to my surprise, it was Ms. Grey on the other end.

"Hi, Mr. Evans. I was just calling to check on you. Before you say anything, I wanted to apologize for my behavior last night. I've never thrown myself on anyone before and I'm sorry for making things strange between us. I never meant to make you uncomfortable."

"You don't have to apologize, Ms. Grey. I'm gonna be honest with you...I don't think you want to get mixed up with someone like me. I ain't got nothin' to offer you and I probably never will. It was for the best that our groove got knocked last night. I wouldn't do anything but cause you problems I'm sure you don't want or need in your life. I don't have the best track record with women and I ain't so hot in my career either. As cliché' as this sounds, it's definitely me and it ain't you," I said, hoping she would understand.

I didn't want to ruin another woman's life and if I kept up this lustful game with Ms. Grey, that's surely what I would do. I would ruin her and she didn't deserve that.

"I understand, Mr. Evans. You have a good weekend and I will see you at work on Monday," she replied weakly. Then she hung up before I could say anything else.

Once again I had undoubtedly hurt another woman. It wasn't my intention to hurt her or anyone else. I figured letting her go now was best for her before things went too far. I lay in my bed wondering what to do next, then my cell phone rang again. I cursed as I answered it blindly.

"Hello."

"May I speak with Dread?"

"This is he. Who's speaking?"

"Neko."

I honestly didn't know what to say. I hadn't spoken to Neko in years and I was surprised that he called.

"Yeah, what can I do for you?" I asked smugly. The last time Neko and I had words they weren't pleasant. He told me to stay away from my own daughter or he would make sure I took an early dirt nap if I didn't. At the time he said those things to me, I was in such a dark place that I had no choice but to adhere to his demands. I knew what he was capable of and I didn't want to meet my demise. Now here he was, years later, calling me.

"I need to talk to you and I can't do it over the phone. Is it possible for us to meet somewhere?"

"Are you sure that's a good idea? I mean...the last time we spoke you said you ain't never wanna see me again and if I got near *my* daughter or your family again, you would have me dealt with," I shot.

"I know what I said and ordinarily I wouldn't be reaching out to you, but there's something I think we need to discuss. It's about YaSheema Nicole."

I perked up hearing my baby girl's name. "Is she... is everything ok?" I asked, growing worried.

"I ain't sure. All I know is that she is in D.C. and I think she may be in trouble. I never thought I would be saying this, but I need your help," Neko said.

"When and where do you want to meet?" I asked, still skeptical about even having a phone conversation with this nigga. He had threatened to take me out and now here he was asking for my help. I couldn't really say no even if I really wanted to. YaSheema was my daughter, and if she needed me, then maybe this was my chance to show and prove that I wasn't as fucked up as I'm sure Neko had made me out to be.

"Meet me at Big Chair Café in Southeast. I'll be there at three. Come alone and don't tell anyone you're meeting me. If you're not there by three, I'm leaving," Neko said and then he hung up.

I sat there holding the phone in my hand with a

bewildered look on my face. Whatever Neko had to tell me couldn't be good. Any news coming from anyone in his family was never good news. The fact that he asked me to come alone was enough to put me on high alert. I didn't trust him and he damn sure ain't trust me. So I'm positive this meeting was going to be nothing nice.

*****

At 2:45, I pulled up in front of Big Chair Café. I sat there watching the dope fiends lining up at the methadone clinic to get their fix for the day. I wondered if I should even be here. Was I truly ready to come face to face with Neko Reynolds? And more importantly, did I want to know what kind of trouble my child was in? I fought the urge to start my car up and back out of the space and never look back. It wouldn't be the first time I had done it. The love I had for my daughter wouldn't allow me to though. I hadn't been there for her for so many years that it was my duty to try and help her if she was in trouble. I may not have been shit before, but maybe now I could try.

I got out of the car and crossed busy Martin Luther King Jr. Avenue and entered the café. I found a seat in the back, but not far off enough that I couldn't get out of there in a hurry if I needed to. From my seat, I could see everyone coming and going. The history I had with this family was enough to make you want to check for all available exits and stay strapped. Nothing good ever came from them. I wasn't a sucker, but anyone associated with them is marked.

I ordered a drink and waited and watched the front door like a hawk. I was good into my drink when I felt someone standing behind me.

"Good to see you, Dread."

I looked behind me and saw Neko standing over me. He took a seat across from me while I wondered where he'd come from. I'd watched the door the whole time and I never saw him enter the place. I shook my head in disbelief. Even when you thought you were being cautious fuckin' with these people, you quickly found out you were slippin'. They were all sneaky and I hope my daughter ain't shit like them. However, I was doubtful. I wouldn't be here right now otherwise.

"Good to see you too," I lied. Seeing Neko couldn't be anything but trouble headed my way.

"Look...we ain't gotta pretend we're the best of friends. Let's be clear, you ain't doing nothin' for me, if you do anything at all. You're doing this for your daughter. In case you forgot who she is, she's the child you left behind. I know back then things were rocky. Believe me, I know. I lost everyone I loved too. You weren't the only one. But I couldn't turn my back on my blood. My niece deserved more than that. My father was notorious for fucking women, dealing drugs, making babies and only raising one of them. Darnell Clayton was a muthafucka'. He created all these mistakes and because of it we all paid the price.

It was like my pops bred and raised craziness. He spoiled YaSheema and raised her to be just like him. She didn't know anything other than what Darnell taught her. She was selfish and stubborn and wante what she wanted or she would take it.

He never raised NiQue and we see how she ended up. She needed my father's attention and love. She needed what my father gave to YaSheema and then to me when he found out about me. Instead, my father concocted a whirlwind of lies and paid people to keep up his charade. He and all the people around him who loved him, paid for it with their lives. I don't want the same thing to happen to my niece. You gotta help stop this cycle. Your daughter may be headed down the same road as her mother. I've seen some shit that leads me to believe she ain't well. I guess I ain't wanna believe that NiQue had passed on the same bad blood to YaSheema Nicole. I tried to ignore it," Neko said.

I looked at him in disbelief. I know this nigga wasn't insinuating that my daughter was crazy. That couldn't be what he was telling me. "What are you saying, Neko? I ain't quite following you."

Neko glared at me so coldly; his eyes told me what I didn't want to face. "Dread, don't play stupid. You know what I'm saying. I don't think I need to spell it out. But in case I do, let me break it down to you like this...the police are looking for your daughter in connection with a murder. I ain't heard shit from her or my wife since she left for school last week.

Something is definitely up with your lil' renegade and if we don't catch up to her, then the police might haul her ass away. I know I don't want that. *If* she ain't seeing things straight, then her being locked up ain't gonna do her no good. She needs some medical attention *if* that's what's going on with her."

My forehead began to sweat and my hands began to tremble uncontrollably. "You said you haven't talked to her since she left for school? She's here isn't she?" I asked, wringing my hands together to stop them from shaking.

"Yeah, she's here. Or at least that's what the school shows. She checked in, but I ain't heard nothin' from her or my wife since..."

"She's here. I saw her. She's enrolled at Howard University; isn't she?" I asked, cutting him off and getting straight to the point.

Neko gave me a peculiar look. "Yeah, she's at Howard. How'd you know? Has she been in touch with you? Has she said anything to you? What did she say?"

"I haven't talked to her. I think I saw her Monday when she was checking in. I think it was her. I tried to catch up to her, but she left the office before I had a chance to talk to her. I knew it was her though. I knew it!" I said panicking.

No parent should be afraid of their flesh and blood. I wasn't afraid, I was terrified. If everything Neko was saying was true, there was no telling what YaSheema

Nicole was up to.

"Keep it down and keep it together. Did she see you?"

I shook my head. I wanted to scream *No,* but the words were caught in my throat. I cleared my throat and stood up.

"Look...good luck on finding her. Good luck on whatever she's mixed up in, but leave me out of it! I'm out of here."

"I knew meeting you and asking you to be a man was asking too much. Any nigga that would walk out on their baby ain't shit!" Neko said standing up.

We were standing face to face and I could see his hatred for me in his eyes. Fuck him! I ain't care what he thought about me.

"You could at least tell me how you knew she was at Howard," Neko said to my back as I walked away.

I stopped and turned to him. "I just started working there and I saw her. Now if you're done, so am I," then I walked out the front door.

Chapter Twenty-Four

Watching my Back
YaSheema Nicole

I don't know why that lady who showed up at my room gave me the creeps, but she did. I swear I remember seeing her somewhere before, but I couldn't put my finger on it. I was probably being paranoid. Takiya had me watching my back about everything.

"You better be glad I got you watching. If I didn't, we would still be in Hick town Upper Marlboro trying to talk some white bitch into giving us a ride back to the mainland. You know what? I never knew you were so gullible," Takiya said, ripping into my consciousness.

"I don't want to hear nothin' else you got to say to me. I know I should have never trusted Lamont and he got away with raping me. We need to just forget about it and move on. It was my mistake," I whispered.

"You're damn right it was your mistake. It was a mistake that could have cost us. I thought *we* were on the same page when *we* came to D.C. I thought we were supposed to be finding *our* father. You've been caught up for a week straight on a nigga who beat you and raped you the first chance he got, and you never once bothered to check on your father. Ain't that the reason *we're* here?"

"No, that ain't the only reason *we're* here. We're supposed to be getting an education," I shot back. Then I picked up the remote control and turned on the television.

I thought my eyes were deceiving me when I came across the five o'clock news. The very same trailer I remembered being in the night before flashed across the screen. I turned the volume up on the television and listened as the reporters stated that the car stolen in last night's crime had been recovered. It was found on the campus of Howard University and the police were dusting it for prints. My mouth hung wide open. I thought *we* had only taken the car. I didn't remember hurting anyone.

"Oh, what did you think? You thought that ole shriveled-up shrew was gonna just give us her car? Fuck no! I took that shit and got *us* home. It's more than what I can say you did. All you fucked around and did was managed to get yourself raped. I saved your stupid ass!"

I put my hands over my ears and tried not to hear what Takiya was saying. Instead of drowning her out, she just got louder. She was insistent upon making me hear her.

"You can cover your ears. You can try to run away all

you want. You can do whatever you like, YaSheema... but I ain't going nowhere. As smart as you are, I would think you would know that by now. Besides what would you do without me? Huh?

"I would be normal. That's what I would do without you. I would have friends. I wouldn't be strange. If it weren't for you, I would probably have my family!" I shouted over the television. I was desperate to get my point across. Takiya had done enough damage and now she was going to know just what I thought of her. "Takiya, I don't need you. Nor do I want you around. I never asked for this. I never asked for any of this! You're driving me crazy and because of you...people are gonna think I'm crazy. You have me committing crimes that I don't remember committing. You're always meddling when you clearly aren't needed! I wish you would just go away!" I screamed.

And just like that there was silence. There was no back talk. Takiya didn't even bother to make a scene. Maybe this time she got the picture and she would just stay gone. I gathered the sweatpants and t-shirt the old woman had given me the night before, stuffed them in a laundry bag and left the room. On my way down to the trash chute, the first thing I noticed was that all the residents were congregating in the lobby. They were all looking out the front door at whatever was going on outside. I inched closer to the group to see what they were all looking at. They were all looking at the three-ring circus of media outside. The reporters were questioning everyone coming and going.

I heard some of the residence chattering. They were all talking about how the police had found the car that was connected in the murder of the old lady. I lowered my head as the guilt consumed me and eased past the onlookers. I had to get rid of these clothes. I didn't need anyone connecting me to any of this mess, so I had to dump them.

I brushed past them all and went out the doors leading outside to the trash chute; I almost walked right into my roommate Paige and Lamont. They were hugged up on one another like old lovers and my blood began to boil watching them interact with one another. I swallowed hard and walked past them like I didn't see either of them.

"Hey, roomie!" I heard Paige call behind me.

I tried to walk faster and pretend I hadn't heard her.

"Hey, YaSheema. Where are you going so fast?" Paige asked.

I whirled around and instead of looking at her, I homed in on Lamont. "I'm going to take out some trash. You know you should be careful of the company you keep. Everyone you think is nice, ain't. There are all kinds of rapist and crazy folks running around this city. I even heard there's a killer on the loose and they may even be right here on campus," I said, mean muggin' Lamont.

Paige looked at me strangely and her eyes followed my gaze. "Oh, I ain't mean to be rude. Lamont this is my roomie, YaSheema Nicole; YaSheema, this is my boyfriend Lamont. He's on the football team and some say my baby is gonna go pro after he graduates this year," Paige said making the awkward introductions. Clearly she didn't know that Lamont and I had met before and no introductions were needed.

Lamont stuck his hand out to shake mine and I refused to shake it. Instead, I coughed in my hand. "Sorry, I think I'm coming down with a cold. Maybe shaking your hand isn't a good idea," I said smugly.

"Maybe not. It's nice meeting you anyway, YaSheema. I'll see you around," Lamont said with a slight smile on his face.

"Yeah...maybe you will," I said and walked off. I dumped the clothes down the chute and headed back inside and wondered if I could trust Paige. I wondered what she would think of her All-Star boyfriend if I told her that he had raped me not even twenty-four hours ago.

When I walked back toward the dorm, I saw Lamont headed toward his car and I don't know what came over me, but I followed him. I was careful to make sure he didn't know I was shadowing him. Luckily for me, I had my keys. When he hopped in his car, I walked a row down to mine and got inside my own vehicle. I watched as he pulled out of the parking lot around all of the police and reporters and I slowly followed behind him, careful not to let him see that I was behind him.

I don't know why I was following him and I didn't know what I was going to do when he got to his destination. I followed him for about five blocks before he pulled up in front of a block of row houses. I parked a few cars behind him and killed my engine as Lamont got out of his car and walked up some steps and fumbled with a set of keys before eventually letting himself inside the house.

I picked the Club up off the floor and separated the interlocking pieces and put the sharp part on the seat next to me. I didn't know what I was going to do with it, but I felt better having it just in case. After waiting for more than an hour, Lamont re-emerged from the house followed by a young woman who was dressed in a pair of ripped jeans and a light jacket. I perked up and got out of the car with the sharp end of the club in my hands and quietly walked to where they had just gotten into the car that I had been raped in the night before. Luckily for me, it was almost dusk and there was no one on the streets. I crept around to the driver's side door of Lamont's car, put the Club behind my back and knocked on the window.

"Excuse me. I hate to bother you kind folks, but my car ran out of gas and I was wondering if you all would be so kind as to give me a lift to a gas station," I yelled through the glass. Lamont looked up and he was startled to see it was me standing there.

The young woman in the passenger seat motioned for him to roll down the window and his punk ass shook his head no. So I took it upon myself to bring the Club up from behind my back and smashed the window in with it. The woman started to yell and Lamont tried to start his car up. Before he could get his keys in the ignition, I took the sharp part of the Club and put all the strength I could behind it and jabbed it in the side of Lamont's neck with absolutely no remorse.

As I roughly yanked the Club out of Lamont's neck, the young broad tried to hop out of the car. I raced around to the passenger side and stopped her before she could fully get her seatbelt off. I held the bloody Club up to her neck and looked her dead in her eyes.

"Your lil' boyfriend...that dead piece of shit over there raped me last night and all I wanted was someone here to like me. Then I found out he was screwing my roommate. And I guess by the looks of that happy look on your face when you walked out arm in arm with his sorry ass, you're fuckin' him too! Well, let me tell you something. You better forget you saw me or I'm coming back for you too. Play with *us*...I mean...me, if you want to and you're gonna wind up dead just like him," I said, pushing the sharp object into the fleshy spot between her neck and shoulder. "Do you understand what I said to you, bitch?" I growled.

The girl shook violently with fear.

"Did you fuckin' hear what I said?" I asked her again, applying more pressure with the Club and drawing blood at the spot where I pressed the weapon.

"Yes! Yes! I heard what you said. I swear I won't

fuckin' tell. I was just fuckin' him! That's all! It ain't anything serious!" the woman said, shaking and crying with fear.

"Well, it ain't nothin' serious for real now, unless you have a thing for dead niggas," I spat back.

"Please just don't kill me!" the woman cried hysterically.

"Today is your lucky day, bitch. You ain't the one I wanted. Now shut the fuck up before you make me kill you!" I said, backing up cautiously. I knew as soon as I turned my back, the bitch was going to either scream or run and I didn't want her to do either until I was in my car and long gone. I never took my eyes off of her until I had backed all the way down the sidewalk and got in my car. Just like I knew her stupid ass would, the girl screamed, breaking the silence on the quiet block. I started the car and sped out off of the street like a bat in hell and never looked back. I don't think I breathed the entire ride back to campus.

Chapter Twenty-Five

For Old Time Sake
Pinky York

After getting Neko the information he needed on his niece and getting the info I needed on Dread, I took my ass home. I was exhausted from playing super sleuth. When I pulled up in front of my house, there was an unfamiliar car parked in my reserved spot and that pissed me off. I was sick of the other residents taking the liberty of parking their cars in my space. I found an empty visitor's spot, parked my car and went inside my building. I waited on the elevator and that's when I saw him.

"You look surprised to see me," Neko chuckled.

"I thought you weren't gonna be here until Monday or Tuesday. Wait, how did you find me? I didn't tell you where I lived and I know I ain't listed," I said, eyeing Neko from head to toe.

"I have my ways of finding who and what I want," he smiled. "Now am I gonna get an invite upstairs or are we gonna stand here in the lobby staring at one another?"

I shook my head and got inside the elevator with Neko right behind me. I don't know why his being so close to me made me so insanely nervous. We got off on my floor and walked down the long corridor to my apartment at the end of the hallway. I could feel Neko's eyes on my backside the entire walk.

Because he was watching me, I put an extra little twist in my hips so he could see exactly what he was missing. He's on my turf now. I opened my door and threw my bag on the coffee table and Neko took a seat on the couch.

"I see things really haven't changed with you. You still love all this pink stuff," he said, taking note of all of my pink décor.

"Yeah...I guess some things never change," I said, lowering my eyes.

Neko patted on the empty space next to him, motioning for me to join him on the couch. I took a seat and got right to the point. "What are you really doing here? I know you ain't track me down to talk about my decorating choices."

"I'ma keep it one hundred with you, Pinky. After seeing you in Georgia, it brought up a lot of old feelings. Old feelings that I thought were dead and buried. I never knew how much I loved you until I lost you. It took a long time for me to get over you. Even after I married Rhina, I still thought of you. You were like the one I let get away. Then you showed up in

Atlanta. I didn't know how to feel and if I was harsh, I'm sorry. Seeing your dead girlfriend is a blow to the system. I guess all this craziness with my niece, Rhina and Dread just has me confused on what's real," he said, taking my hand in his.

Did he just say Dread? I thought to myself.

"Well, were you able to find out any more information on your niece other than what I gave you? And what about Dread?" I asked him hoping he wouldn't see my eagerness to get as much info on Dread as I possibly could. Neko had motives and so did I.

"I went to meet Dread. I needed him to step up and be a father to his daughter. If YaSheema is going through even half the shit I think she may be going through, she is gonna need all the love and support she can get."

"Neko, I don't get it. I ain't following you. I know about the police back in Georgia, but what else is wrong?" I asked curiously. Neko shifted around on the couch uncomfortably and I don't know why, but I regretted asking him anything.

"Do you remember the last time we spoke before we got separated? You were supposed to come see me. Well, that night I was almost killed holding YaSheema Nicole in my arms. Her mother tried to blow our heads off. NiQue let a bunch of cats out the bag that night. She told me that she was really my sister. She told me that my pops was her father too. NiQue told me that

Darnell had kept her a secret because she wasn't up to his standards."

My mouth fell open. I knew Darnell was grimy and an ass chaser; hell, I had even given my former boss some pussy before, but I never figured that NiQue was his daughter too. Sure she was always around, but I would have never suspected that she was more than YaYa's best friend.

"What do you mean *not up to his standards*?" I asked.

"NiQue had multiple personality disorder. She was so far gone that she was listening to the voice or voices–since I don't know how many were really there–in her head. She went on a killing rampage and any and every one she thought could get in her way or found out her secret, she was after them. That included me. She was knocking niggas off in an attempt to keep Dread from finding out that she was a nutcase. She would rather go on killing than getting the help she needed because she feared being locked up in an institution. That night you were supposed to come over, NiQue showed up and she tried to kill me. She didn't look like herself and you could tell she was struggling with something stronger than herself. Her voice was different and she called herself another name. She called herself Pajay."

"Wait you mean the sister that killed YaYa? So you mean to tell me that NiQue was Pajay?" I interrupted. I couldn't help it. I was trying to piece it all together.

"Yes. She was one and the same. My father didn't

want anything to do with NiQue...or Pajay because she was dangerous. He saw her as a liability, but he couldn't completely rid himself of her. That wasn't his style. He kept her around, but hoped she would never find out the truth about who she really was. NiQue was really Darnell's first born child that he had with my aunt. Apparently, there was something wrong with their DNA makeup and it made NiQue crazy as fuck, and now I think that nasty trait has been passed along to my niece," Neko said, putting his hands in his head.

I inched closer to him and rubbed my hand along his leg for reassurance. "Well, why don't you contact the authorities so they can lock her up? She might be a danger to someone or herself," I suggested. I thought it was all very simple.

"What if she is just as gone as her mother was? She ain't gonna be nothin' nice if she is. Actually, I think she's already on her way off the deep end. I still ain't heard anything from my wife and it's been a whole week. That ain't like Rhina, so I know YaSheema Nicole has something to do with my wife's disappearance."

I sat there dumbfounded. The young woman I had seen earlier today didn't seem like she could hurt anyone. She seemed aggravated that I had knocked on her door, but I didn't think she would be capable of murdering anyone. But who was I to judge? I had off'ed many a nigga and no one ever suspected shit. I learned to never judge a book by its cover.

"Pinky, I don't expect you to believe or understand what I'm telling you, but I do want you to hear me out. I ain't dealing with a teenager with an attitude. I came here to tell you these things so that if something happens to me, at least one person knows the truth and can get her the help she needs."

"Neko, you don't think she would hurt you, do you?" I asked, growing concerned. I had just come face to face with her only a little while ago. Had I put my life in danger trying to help Neko?

"I honestly don't know, Pink. I could be worried about nothing, but I got that sinking feeling I'm not." Neko looked deeply in my eyes and I saw how afraid he really was and I was actually afraid for him.

"So, what's next?" I asked, looking away. I didn't want to get caught up in Neko's world only to be dropped off the side of a cliff when his wife returned; if she ever returned.

Neko let go of my hand and held my face cupped in his strong hands.

"Whatever happens from here, Pinky, I wanted you to know I love you. I never stopped loving you."

Then Neko kissed me. I didn't pull away from him like I knew I should; instead, I hungrily kissed him back. His hands roamed underneath the cotton shirt I was wearing and he gently pinched my nipples. I let out a moan and relished in Neko's familiar touch. It had been seventeen long years since Neko had touched me like the way he was touching me now and my body greatly missed him.

"Are you sure you want to do this, Neko?" I managed to mumble through his frantic kisses. I didn't want him to leave me again; not because of death and not because of another woman. I needed him to be sure I was what he wanted. He had to be sure because there was no going back once we crossed this line again.

"I'm sure," Neko moaned in my ear causing my womanhood to throb in anticipation of what it had been missing all this time. That was all I needed to hear before I slid back just a little and pulled my t-shirt over my head and tossed it on the floor.

Neko swooped me up in his arms, laid me down and went to work on body. He kissed each scar I had been ashamed of and so much more. I tried to cover up and he quickly stopped me.

"I want to see all of you. Pink, ain't no scar or anything else that can make me feel any different about you," With that, he pulled down my jeans and kissed each scar until he made his way down between my thighs and moved my lacy, pink boy shorts to the side and stuck his fingers in my honeypot. He about drove me insane when he pulled his fingers out, licked them and said, "Yeah...ain't shit changed."

After that, we made love until the sun came up over D.C. the next morning.

Chapter Twenty-Six

Bad News is Always Hard to Swallow
Neko

I woke up to the sound of my cell phone chirping to let me know I had a text. I rolled over and saw Pinky lying beside me and this is where a nigga belonged. This is what I had been missing; her. Gently, I eased away from her so I wouldn't disturb her while she was sleeping and checked my messages. It was Shadow and I had a voicemail message from some strange 804 area code. I checked the message from Shadow which was vague and only told me to call him ASAP. Instead of checking the voicemail, I opted to call Shadow first because the 804 call had to be a wrong number or a sales call. I dialed Shadow's number and he answered on the first ring.

"What's up, my nigga? Is everything aight?" I said quietly as soon as he answered.

"I don't know if everything is aight, but I got news on your folks. I spoke with my niece Paige and you're never gonna believe this shit. Paige and YaSheema

Nicole are roommates," Shadow explained.

I was glad to hear that YaSheema Nicole was okay, but I knew Shadow wasn't done giving me the low down yet.

"There's something else, Neko. There have been two murders linked to the campus in the last two days. There was a murder of some old woman in Upper Marlboro and her car was found on the student parking lot; and there was a murder of a student that occurred last night. The police are saying the two incidents may be related. Apparently from what I was able to get from Paige, the student murdered was killed in his car. The dude was Paige's boyfriend of the last two years. Man, Paige is fucked up about losing him. They were supposed to get married after he graduated this year. He was a senior and he was a star football player that was rumored to be getting drafted after he finished college. I met him for the first time last year. He was a nice kid. From what Paige could tell me through her hysterical crying, there was a witness. He was with some female a few blocks away from the campus and from what the girl was able to tell the police, she and Lamont were attacked by a young woman with grey eyes."

That was all I needed to hear. It confirmed my worst fear. My niece was out of control. Sure, I haven't seen any of it for myself, but I really didn't need too. The scenario was the same as it was once before. My niece was headed down a path of destruction and I was gonna have to stop her before she hurt anyone else or herself.

"Thanks, Shadow. Look...do me a favor, tell Paige to come home right now. If my niece is up to half of the shit I think she may be up to, then your daughter may not be safe. Tell her to come home and stay as far away from YaSheema Nicole as she possibly can," I warned.

"What the fuck is going on, Neko? I know you ain't trying to tell me your shawty did all of that shit," Shadow asked.

"I ain't got time to talk about it. Just do what I told you and get your daughter out of there! I'll swing by your house after I have Pinky take me to the campus. I've got to get to YaSheema Nicole before the police get to her."

"Aight, man and no worries. Paige said she can't focus. She's supposed to pack a few things and come home. She says she can't be on campus right now. She said it's like a media circus around there and she wanted to come home for a few days. Call me once you make a move, my nigga and Neko...be careful. One," Shadow said and disconnected the call.

I immediately started putting on my clothes. Me keeping quiet and not waking Pinky was out the window. She was sitting up in the bed with her big doe eyes watching me scramble around her room to find my long since discarded clothes.

"What's happening, Neko? Where are you going?

Is everything aight?" she asked me worried.

"Baby, you should go back to sleep and I promise I'll be back. I've gotta handle what I came here to handle."

"Talk to me, Neko. What happened?" Pinky said growing increasingly distressed. She threw the covers back, hopped out of the bed and started searching around for her clothes.

"Oh, no. You're staying here. I just found you and I ain't gonna let nothin' come between us again. If anything were to happen to you I would lose it," I said, stopping Pinky in her tracks. I wasn't about to let her fight this fight for me. This was something I had to do myself. I had to step up and take care of my seed. She may not have been mine by biologically, but YaSheema Nicole was my responsibility. She was my blood. She was a bad seed and it was time for me to be the man she needed me to be. It was time for me to break the cycle that haunted and hunted my family for so long. It was time for me to end the Clayton-Reynolds curse.

"Neko, you already know I ain't gonna' let you go at this shit alone. Some people never get a second chance at life. We did and I ain't gonna let you walk out that door without me. If you're gonna go down...I'm going down with you. You can argue all you want, but I ain't even trying to hear it. So either you take me with you or you ain't going," she said. Her face was screwed up and I knew she meant business. That's why I loved Pinky; she was a straight rider. Even in her older age, she is still down for me no matter what.

"Pinky, there were two murders and I think YaSheema Nicole had something to do with them both. This shit could get ugly. She may even get angry as soon as she sees you with me. She'll know you told me where she was. I can't risk her turning on you," I said, trying to talk her out of coming with me.

"Neko, maybe you forgot who I really am. This is something slight. We go over there, get her and take her to a hospital. It's simple."

I'm glad she was convinced it was going to be that easy because I sure wasn't. I don't know why I gave in to her. I really don't think I had much of a choice because Pinky was either coming with me or she wasn't going to let me out the door. I nodded my head at her and she snatched up her clothes and went to the bathroom. I finished getting dressed and picked up my cell phone again. I was going to give Dread one last call and let him know he should lay low even though I didn't owe him shit since he didn't want to man up and be a father to his wayward child.

I scrolled through my call log and found his number and left him a message letting him know something had happened to YaSheema and I needed him to meet me at the school. I gave him the dorm info I had gotten from Pinky, even though I didn't know if he was going to meet me or not, but it was worth a shot to ask. Either he would or he wouldn't. No matter what, I had to. After leaving him a voicemail message, I saw the blinking icon on my phone letting me know I had a message waiting for retrieval. A cold chill ran up my spine as I listened to the message from the Richmond, Virginia Police Department telling me to call them right away. I punched in the number that the caller, Detective Bines, left on the message. He answered on the first ring.

"This is Detective Bines."

"Detective Bines, this is Neko Reynolds. You left me a message."

"Yes, sir. I'm with the Richmond Police Department. Is there any way you can come to the precinct?"

"Detective Bines, I am in no position to get to Richmond. I am about two hours from Richmond in Washington, D.C. Do you mind telling me what this is about? I'm kind of pressed for time," I said, pulling my shoes on and surfing through my pockets for my car keys.

"Sir, I hate to tell you this over the phone and it really isn't our protocol to do things of this nature over the phone. I think it would be best if you came in and spoke with me. The issue is of a sensitive nature."

"Detective, either you can tell me over the phone or you will be waiting for quite some time before you tell me anything at all. I have a situation I'm in the middle of that requires my immediate attention," I said sternly.

"Mr. Reynolds, again I apologize for having to tell you something like this over the phone but you're leaving me no choice. We believe we have located the remains of your wife, Rhina Diaz-Reynolds."

The whole room started to instantly spin. I know I didn't hear this man tell me he had found my wife's remains.

"Wait a minute. Her remains as in..."

"Yes, Mr. Reynolds, her body was found decomposing in a hotel room in Richmond, Virginia. She died of multiple stab wounds and she's been in the room for quite some time. Sir, we would like to ask you a few questions to help us find out who did this and why. Do you think you could come in and assist us?"

I sunk back on the bed and tried to digest what I'd heard. The tears started to pour and when Pinky walked in the room, she took one look at me and rushed to my side. I swallowed the bile and pressed the phone to my ear.

"Are you sure it's her? I mean...how could she be dead in a hotel for damn near a week and no one know anything? Why hadn't anyone gone in to check on her? Where were the maids...housekeeping...anyone?" I yelled into the phone with my voice cracking more and more with each word as the reality of what was happening to me sunk in.

"Apparently, someone had put the *Do not disturb* sign on the door and has been paying for the room by phone to keep anyone from finding out she was in there by way of her credit cards.. It wasn't until the guests of the hotel noticed a funny smell coming from the room before the hotel staff gained access to the room and found her. Mr. Reynolds is there anyone who would want to hurt your wife?" the detective asked.

Pinky stood there watching me like a hawk. She didn't know what was being said to me, but I'm sure she knew it wasn't good.

"Detective, I've got an idea who may have done it, but you have to give me time to figure it out. I'll be on my way to Richmond tonight," I said.

"Mr. Reynolds, if you have any information we would need you to give it to us so we can put this person away. Whoever did this is…excuse me for being so frank…is a sick fuck and I want nothing more than to put them behind bars. I need your help to do that…"

Before he could finish his plea, I had hung up the phone on him. I had heard enough. I couldn't take anymore. Pinky stood over me with a mixture of curiosity and sadness in her eyes.

"Neko…if you don't want to tell me, you don't have to," she said sincerely.

"YaSheema Nicole killed my wife and left her body in Richmond," I croaked out.

"Oh my God, Neko. I'm so sorry. I mean…I don't know what to say…"

"Don't say anything, Pinky. You don't have to be sorry. You don't have to say anything at all. Just get your gun and let's go!" I said, standing up and walking toward the door.

It was time to end this shit once and for all no matter how bad it hurt.

Chapter Twenty-Seven

Full Throttle
Dread

I saw that Neko had called and left me a message. He was probably cursing me out for not helping him with YaSheema Nicole. He was just gonna have to understand I ain't ready to deal with her or any of them for that matter. All of the members of that family, including my daughter, were tainted. I was trying to pull myself out of the abyss I had fallen into since meeting any of them and no one was going to pull me back in. I really didn't care if it was my daughter. I wanted to make things right between her and me, but doing so could cause me more harm than good.

Against my better judgment, I listened to the voice-mail anyway. Just as I suspected, Neko was attempting to call me in as reinforcement. I didn't know what he didn't understand. Actually, I was glad that he had met up with me and warned me about my daughter. There was no telling what could have happened if I ran into her on campus. For all I know, she could have been a complete psycho like her mother. That's exactly why I was never going back to that school again. I ain't give a fuck what Queen, Crack, or Ms. Grey had to say about it.

There was a knock on my door that jolted me from my private thoughts. I was on edge just knowing the people I feared the most were in D.C., and the one who could cause me the most harm was looking for me. I started to panic, wondering who was at my door. Even though Crack and Queen lived in a gated and secured community, I didn't trust any of it. I picked up a baseball bat off the floor, eased to the door and peered through the peephole. My heart rate only returned to normal when I saw Queen on the other side of the door. She began to knock harder.

"I know you're in there. Open the door, Dread. I can hear you moving around in there so I know your ass is home. Now open up the damn door!" Queen demanded.

I unlocked the door and opened it and let her in.

"Damn, what are you doing in here? I know you heard me knocking. What's with the bat? You planning on playing baseball or somethin'?" Queen asked me, eying the bat.

"Naw. I just thought...never mind. What do you need, Queen?" I asked, trying not to let her annoy me. I knew she was going to be pissed once she found out I was quitting the job she had gotten me.

"I was just coming to check on you, that's all. Can't I come and check on you?" she asked playfully.

I looked at her sideways and rolled my eyes. Queen was a sweetheart when she wanted to be, but the problem was her sarcastic ass never wanted to be a sweetheart. All five feet of her was a ball of fire and always had been since Crack and I were kids.

"Since when did you start checking on me? You only come around when you want your rent money or to harass me about sleeping in the carport or finding liquor bottles in the pool. Since I ain't been in the pool and I went to sleep in my own bed last night, you ain't got anything to check on me about Queen. I'm good," I said frustrated.

"Look...I ain't the one who went to bed with you last night so you ain't got no reason to be snapping on me. Now, do you want to tell me what's wrong or am I gonna have to take that bat and beat it out of you?" Queen said rolling her neck.

I dropped the bat and put my hands up as if I were surrendering.

"You got it, Queen. I don't want any trouble. I ain't mean to snap on you either, sis. I just got some heavy shit on my mind and I gotta make a few changes. Some of the changes are ones you and my boy ain't gonna like but I have to do it," I said, taking a seat in my recliner.

Queen lifted her eyebrow and I knew I had said way too much to her. I knew she was never going to leave until she found out what I was talking about.

"Ok, Dread...spill it. I've known you too long. I know something is going on," she said, pulling one of the folding chairs out.

"I'm not going back to the school to work for Ms. Grey. Shit is kind of complicated."

"You fucked her didn't you? I told you to keep things on a professional level. Damn, Dread! All you had to do was keep your dick in your pants and collect a check. How hard is that?" she sighed. She looked disappointed in me and I didn't like it.

"No! Despite what you think, I didn't sleep with Ms. Grey. I ain't saying I didn't want to, but I didn't fuck her. I almost fucked her but it didn't go down like that. I got bigger fish to fry besides fucking your friend, Ms. Grey. I'm not going back because I just found out my daughter is there," I said, wishing I had a drink. I sure needed it for the way this conversation was going. Queen cocked her head to the side like she hadn't heard me correctly.

"I know I ain't hearing this shit right. Your daughter attends Howard? How do you even know it's her? It's not like you've seen her since..." her voice trailed off. Maybe Queen knew she was overstepping the boundaries. In my personal opinion, she definitely was.

"I know it's her because her uncle told me it was her. She attends college at Howard University full-time now and unfortunately, she's been looking for me for a few years according to Neko. I guess she came here in hopes of finding me," I sighed.

"Well, that's great then. You can get reacquainted with your daughter. I know you really want that," Queen said excitedly.

"No, that's what *she* wants. I want her to stay the hell away from me. You don't get it. She's looking for me for the wrong reasons. She might wanna take my fuckin head off. She came here to get at me...not to have a family reunion. Nothing good can come from us meeting."

Queen shifted around in her chair and I could see she was slightly uncomfortable for making a bad assumption. She didn't know what was going on in my life. How could she? I hardly ever spoke to her and Crack anymore. Even when they tried, I shut them out.

"Why do you think she would want to harm you, Dread?" she inquired.

"Are you fuckin' kidding me? Why wouldn't she want to kill me is a more fitting question. What kind of father have I been to her? She probably wouldn't know me if I was standing directly in front of her. By the way...I was standing in front of her and she didn't know who I was. I've missed every birthday, every holiday and I abandoned her when her mother died... out of fear. Why wouldn't she want to kill me?"

"You sound silly! I think she would benefit from knowing you. You have to let her know it wasn't her fault that you left. You have to explain it to her so that she understands that you left her because you had no choice. I'm sure once you sit down with her face to face and explain your side of things, she will get it. She may be upset at first, but if she is anything like you, she will forgive."

"Sit down with her? Who's to say she would even allow me that chance?" I asked sadly.

"You will never know unless you reach out to her and try and find out," Queen said, standing up.

"As for you quitting...I understand. I don't like it and I expect that you will be on a job hunt shortly."

I nodded my head in her direction even though I had no intention on looking for another job. Working is what got me in this shit in the first place; but I had to at least humor Queen and tell her I would look or she would never stop breathing down my neck.

"Good. I'll even call Ms. Grey and tell her you won't be returning for personal reasons." Queen said, heading to the door.

"Naw. I'll tell Ms. Grey on my own. I think I owe her at least that."

"Dread, I want you to think about the opportunities that have all been laid out in front of you. It ain't coincidental. It was pre-ordained. You know I ain't a holy roller, but I do believe there is something more powerful than us strategizing our moves. Our stories have already been written. It's just our job to read the pages and live out the part that was written for us. There are no do-overs and you can't change what has already been written; but I think you change how the story ultimately ends. I just don't want you to miss out on your chance to get your story right. It started off promising, and then there was gloom and doom. Now, maybe you can get to that fantastic twist that even you weren't expecting."

Then she opened the door and took one last look at me and I nodded at her. I understood what she was saying. Then she slipped quietly out of the front door.

Not even five minutes after she'd left, I raced outside to my car. It was past time for me to get my story right. Or at the very least, tell my side of things.

I got in the car and headed to Howard University to make amends with my daughter. It was long overdue and I think it's high time that she and I met. I just hoped that she was nothing like her mother and that when our introductions were over, I could live to tell about the experience.

Chapter Twenty-Eight

Renegade
YaSheema Nicole/Takiya

I thought I would feel better after killing Lamont, but I didn't. I've been holed up in my dorm since I jabbed him in his throat with the Club. I was afraid to leave the room because I had fucked up royally. I left someone alive. As much as I hated to admit that Takiya was much savvier at handling situations like these, she really was.

"Oh, so you're admitting that you can't do this without me; huh? Oh and yes, you were stupid for not killing that bitch. You should have cut that bitch's throat wide open. But no...you let her go. You let her ass go based upon a promise that she obviously ain't gonna keep. If you believed she was gonna keep her promise you wouldn't be hiding out in the pissy room like a coward. Had you killed her like I would've, she would have been nothing more than an afterthought. Now you got a fuckin' problem!" Takiya chuckled.

"I'm glad you think this shit is funny. I don't see shit

worth laughing about. If I'm fucked, so are you or did you forget?" I sighed, burying my head in the pillow to ignore Takiya, but she was far from done with me. She was on one and she wasn't about to let up either.

"I think we should go back to see lil' miss hot ass and finish her. If we don't, she can identify you. I'm sure you've noticed the police have been crawling around this muthafucka' all night because of you and your stupidity."

"They were here anyway, or did you forget? They were here because you wanna knock off lil' ole white ladies and steal cars like you're a damn Dukes of Hazard!" I shouted.

"Don't you think you should keep it down before your roomie finds out you killed her lil' love bug? God help us if she cries one more God damn tear today. If she only knew what a piece of shit that Lamont character was, she wouldn't be wasting those tears on him."

"Damn, Takiya I wish you would shut the fuck up; I'm trying to figure out what to do next since you ain't tryna' help. All you wanna do is tell me how badly I fucked up. So if you ain't gonna help me, then I wish you would get the fuck on!" I screamed. That's when my dorm door swung open and in walked Paige. I could still hear Takiya ranting, but I had to try to act as though everything was cool. I had done more than enough damage. I didn't need to get caught talking to myself.

"Hi, Paige. Can I get you anything?" I stammered.

"I swear you can't do shit right! Why are you making nice with that sniffling bitch? Just stay quiet and leave her ass alone. If she doesn't say anything to us, then we shouldn't be saying anything to her!" Takiya warned me.

"Were you on the phone, YaSheema? I swore I heard you talking to someone right before I walked in," Paige asked, doing a full scan of the room.

"Ahh....it may have been the radio," I lied.

Paige looked at me strangely. "How are you listening to the radio and it ain't even plugged up?"

"Ahh....umm..."

See, I told you, you are a royal fuck up. Where would you be without me; huh? Probably sitting in a padded room in one of those hospitals being poked and prodded like some science project. I swear you are worthless as a penny with a hole in it. Takiya scolded me.

I did my best to tune Takiya out and focus on Paige, but Takiya was doing a good job of making sure that didn't happen.

"I guess I'm a lil' shook up with everything happening around here," I managed to mumble. I was addressing Paige, but Takiya once again barged in as if I was addressing her.

Blah, blah, blah. Why are you still making small talk with this bitch? This time I couldn't ignore her. This time I slipped up.

"Will you shut the fuck up and get the fuck out!" I screamed, covering my ears and startling Paige. She dropped the bag she was packing and looking at me strangely.

"I'm sorry, Paige. I didn't mean you. I meant..."

"I'm the only one here, YaSheema. Who else are you talking to?" Paige said, backing away from me.

I could see the fear in her eyes and it was written all over her weary face. I felt that same feeling I felt before; that same hazy feeling where my body felt heavy and weighted down. I knew what was happening to me, but there was nothing I could do to stop it. Takiya was looking for a reason to show her ass and she decided now was the time to do so. The more I struggled to suppress her, the more enraged she became until I couldn't fight her anymore and everything around me went black.

Are you afraid, bitch? Well, guess what...you should be. If I were you, I would be afraid.

"YaSheema, I don't know what's going on with you, but you're starting to scare me," Paige managed to squeak.

"Aww, you are afraid. Let me tell you what you should have really been afraid of. You should have been afraid of that limp dick loser you called your boyfriend. I tried to warn YaSheema about him, but she didn't listen. I tried to tell her not to go out with him, but she didn't listen. And do you know where that got her? It got her raped and left out in the stix with some selfish ass white bitch who didn't wanna even give *us* a ride. All *we* wanted was a god damn ride and the lil' ole bitch wouldn't give *us* a ride!"

"YaSheema, why are you talking to yourself in third person and what does Lamont have to do with any of this?" Paige said, easing backwards toward the bathroom.

"YaSheema? Oh, that silly bitch! She checked out and sweetie I checked in. It's nice to meet you. Oh, and as for that boyfriend of yours...yeah I killed that stupid nigga. He deserved everything I gave him and so much more. Had YaSheema followed my instructions, you would have never found out that I killed him. She's such a fuck up. I swear I spend more time cleaning up her messes than anything else."

"Bitch, you're crazy! I'm getting the fuck out of here," Paige said right before she made an attempt to snatch her cell phone and make a dash for the bathroom. Before she could close the door, *we* were right on her heels. She struggled to close the door, but *we* were stronger and faster then she anticipated. *We* pushed on the door, hitting our target square in the nose with the heavy wood door with all of *our* strength and knocked Paige backwards into the sink. Blood was spewing and she was screaming and pleading for *us* to spare her.

"Don't run from *us*, bitch. You're gonna make this more difficult than it has to be," *we* threatened.

Paige was so scared, she couldn't move even if she wanted to. That's when *we* hit her again and spun her around to face the mirror and grabbed a fistful of her hair.

"Don't you wanna see it?" we asked Paige who was sobbing hysterically and bleeding heavily from her nose. Paige closed her eyes as if to spite *us* and that pissed *us* off even more.

"I said look, bitch!"

When Paige refused to open her eyes, *we* slammed her head into the glass mirror that hung over the small sink. Paige crashed to the floor. Grabbing her by her hair again, I dragged her like a caveman to the toilet and lifted the lid.

"Too bad you came home when you did. If you hadn't come home, you might've had a chance roomie."

Paige was completely limp, but she was still breathing. I couldn't let her live now. If *we* let her live, there was no doubt in our mind that she would snitch on *us* if *we* were to let her live. *We* pushed her head in the bowl and slammed the lid down on her neck. *We* could hear her neck snapping in several places from the force of the lid clobbering her. When *we* got tired, *we* decided *we* had had enough fun playing with Paige. *We* pushed her head completely in the bowl and held her there until *we* felt her entire body go limp and *we* were satisfied that she was dead.

"See, now that's how you handle shit. You never leave anyone behind that can tell on *us*. Now, let's get the fuck out of here before someone comes looking for this bitch."

We scooped our keys up off of the dresser and anything *we* could find of value and *we* left. *We* would never be able to get Paige out of the room without being detected, so it was time for *us* to saddle up and ride out. *We* weren't gonna be caught with the smoking gun. *We* stuffed whatever *we* could take in a bag and took off.

Chapter Twenty-Nine

The Showdown
Neko, Dread, Pinky, YaSheema Nicole, Takiya

When we pulled up at the college, I was surprised to see Dread. He had just pulled up and parked next to my car. I don't think Pinky saw him yet and I don't know how she's going to react when she finally sees him. They had so much bad blood between them from years past that it was still thick.

"Pinky, I don't know how to tell you this, but we have company. I don't want you to freak out, but I called in some reinforcement."

Pinky looked out of the window and her eyes immediately landed on Dread getting out of his car. A sneaky smile curled on her lips and I instantly knew I had made a huge mistake by calling him and leaving him that voicemail message. I didn't think he was really going to come and assist me in getting his daughter the help she needed. Now I had more than one issue to handle.

I reached over and grabbed Pinky's arm right before

she got out of the car, “He’s here to help, Pinky. Don’t do anything you’re gonna regret. Do you hear me?”

Pinky’s eyes were fixated on Dread and her wicked smile widened. “I hear you, but I can’t make you any promises. Do you know how long I have waited for this moment? Do you know how long I’ve wanted to blow his fuckin head off? Then you give him to me in a pretty lil’ bow and then you tell me I can’t have him? Naw, Neko...I don’t think I’m gonna be able to do it. I missed my mark seventeen years ago and I will not miss this time,” Pinky said practically drooling.

I watched as she slid her hand inside her pink Coach bag. When her hand reappeared, she was holding her gun in her left hand and caressing it with her right.

“Pinky, I ain’t gonna let you do something you’re gonna regret. Let’s just handle what we came here...”

Before I could finish my statement, I saw YaSheema Nicole dart from the building we were parked in front of. Then she quickly scanned the parking lot and headed in the direction of the parked cars and straight for Rhina’s Benz. My niece looked around nervously before she got in and cranked up the car.

I knew if I didn’t react, she could easily disappear again and I couldn’t afford to have that happen again. I was here and this was now or never. Pinky was so preoccupied with Dread that she never saw my niece trying to make a break for it. I knew I had to take matters into my own hands or things could go terribly wrong. I jumped out of the car and ran to her car and banged on the window causing YaSheema Nicole to jump.

"Get out of the car, YaSheema," I said, trying to remain calm. I remembered the last time I was in this position and I had always wished I could have done more to save my sister. This time I was going to save my niece. I was going to save her from herself before she did any more damage.

"Uncle Neko? What are you doing here?" YaSheema asked me, blinking her eyes to make sure she was seeing what she thought she saw.

"Yes, baby girl...it's me," I said nervously. That's when I heard footsteps coming from behind me.

"YaSheema," I heard Dread call out.

"Uncle Neko, who is that?" she asked me.

"That's...he's what you've been searching for. That's your father," I said, feeling out of place as the two of them stared each other up and down. YaSheema Nicole wrinkled up her nose as if something smelled bad.

"This nigga ain't my daddy. My daddy left me with you and as far as I am concerned that nigga is dead." YaSheema spat.

I noticed the small spots of what appeared to be blood that covered the front of her pink top and my heart sank. I knew she had done something else and we hadn't gotten there in enough time to stop her. "YaSheema, you can't hold on to the hatred you feel for your father. You wanted to know for so long who he was and now is your chance. This is your chance to make amends with him," I said, hoping that she would be reasonable. She started cringing and smacking herself which caused me to jump back. She covered her ears and began to scream out words which I couldn't understand. I went to reach out for her and she looked at me with so much built up anger and hate that I fell back. I had seen that look before. I had seen it when I encountered her mother on the night the police stopped NiQue from killing me and YaSheema Nicole both. I knew right then I wasn't dealing with YaSheema anymore. I didn't know who I was dealing with and I was scared to find out.

"Unc, I advise you to keep your hands to your fucking self unless you wanna end up like good ole Auntie Rhina."

Hearing her admit to what she'd done was too much for me to bear. The little girl who I had raised as my own was no longer there. She had been replaced by this thing standing in front of me with her face twisted up and her hand in her pockets searching for God only knew what.

"Baby, I'm sorry I haven't been there for you. I just didn't know what to do. I was grieving. I lost your mother and your aunt in the matter of months. I was confused, YaSheema. Please just give me a chance to make things right. Give me a chance to do the right thing," Dread pleaded as he moved closer to YaSheema Nicole who was still trying to find whatever it was that she was looking for. However, she never took her eyes off of me and Dread as she searched feverishly in her pocket. Then all of a sudden, she stopped searching and homed in on Dread. She blinked as if she were trying to see clearly. "Daddy?"

"Yes, baby it's me and I promise I won't ever leave you again. I swear I won't," he said, moving closer to her. Before I could tell him not too, everything started to move in slow motion. YaSheema Nicole smiled a wicked smile that only I saw. She reached in her back pocket as her father went to hug her and she pulled a knife from behind her. With one swift motion, she took the blade to Dread's neck.

I watched in shock and horror as he stumbled backwards holding the incision across his neck in attempts to stop the blood that was gushing. Dread dropped to his knees and rolled over on his side. I rushed to him to see if I could help him. The hospital was located right across from the campus. I turned back toward the car and yelled for Pinky to call 911. In the two seconds it all took for it to come to this, YaSheema Nicole was standing over me with malice in her eyes.

"Unc, you should have let me do this shit years ago and maybe *we* would have turned out a lil' better than this. Sorry it had to be this way," she said as she lifted the blade high in the air. There was no time to stop her or protest before three shots rang out. I could hear the sound of the hot lead whizzing by me and catching my niece with three shots to the chest, center mass.

I watched as my niece, the last of my bloodline, fell over on the concrete beside the man who created her. I looked behind me to see Pinky standing there with her gun in her hands and tears streaming down her tired face. She lowered her weapon as I focused my attention on YaSheema Nicole and scooped her up in my arms; rocking her like a newborn baby. Her breathing was shallow and ragged and if she didn't get some attention soon she was going to die.

I could hear the sirens in the distance and Pinky ran to my side. "Neko, I'm...I'm sorry I didn't know what else to do. I saw the knife and if I didn't react, she was going to kill you. I didn't have a choice," Pinky said, explaining why she had done it. She was barely audible because I was still holding on to my niece tightly; hoping the blaring sounds of the ambulance would be upon us soon.

"Hold on YaSheema Nicole. Hold on dammit! Help is on the way!" I screamed. Her eyes popped open and I couldn't believe it. I looked at my niece in amazement as she clung on to life for a second longer.

"Uncle Neko, I'm sorry. I'm so sorry...for everything. I didn't mean for anyone to get hurt. It's just that Takiya... she wanted to do things her way...I didn't mean to hurt you, Unc, but it's better this way. I can be with my parents now...I love you," YaSheema Nicole said and then she took her last breath and died right there in my arms.

Epilogue

Eternal
Neko

The end of a dark legacy ended the day my niece died. Even though I would have done anything to save her, I couldn't. Maybe it was better that way. All YaSheema Nicole wanted was her parents and I figure she finally got them. The very night she died, I felt like a weight was lifted from my soul. I knew my entire family had found peace in death's arms and now it was time for me to start living my life as though each day were my last. Being related to them taught me that.

Pinky accompanied me to Richmond, Virginia to identify my wife's body and we laid YaSheema, Rhina and Dread to rest in the city they loved along with my mother, sisters and my father. My nigga, Shadow was fucked up over the death of his daughter. He blamed me for it. It was fucked up how they found her. I couldn't blame Shadow for wanting to keep his distance.

Crack and Queen keep in touch from time to time. They even told me that Dread's album topped the charts. Maybe there was some sunshine after all this rain. Too bad he became a big star after his death; but I guess that's just how the cookie crumbles.

I wonder on a daily basis what would have happened if I would have never ignored the signs that were definitely there? What if I had gotten YaSheema Nicole the help she needed? Maybe with treatment, she would have been a normal, healthy, stable young lady and we wouldn't have had to bury some many innocent people. I definitely blame myself.

I knew God had marked my family and I hoped the plague of lies, deceit and betrayal had all ended with the bloodshed that day on the campus of Howard University. I try not to think about the tragedies I had to endure. That's why I want no part of the book Pinky is writing. I want to support my new wife on her writing ventures, but reliving the past was something I never wanted to do. Pinky said she understood and that she had to write the book for her own reasons. Who was I to stop her? She said it was her way of coping with everything. She even has a publisher that she met in Georgia by the name of George Sherman Hudson who was willing to publish the series for her. She'd met him when she was searching for me. I hope these books give her what she needs. I have to admit the title is kind of catchy and I think with all the craziness she is writing about, it should be a *New York*

Times bestseller. I think her series, Dirty DNA, will be a big hit. Too bad the real characters aren't here to see its birth. But I guess that's the way it was meant to be...

The End.

We'd like to thank you for supporting G Street Chronicles
and invite you to join our social networks.
Please be sure to post a review when you're finished
reading.

Like us on Facebook
G Street Chronicles
G Street Chronicles CEO Exclusive Readers Group

□ollo□ us on □□itter
@GStreetChronicl

□ollo□ us on □nsta□ra□
gstreetchronicles

Email us and we'll add you to our mailing list
fans@gstreetchronicles.com

George Sherman Hudson, CEO
Shawna A., COO